SHUDDERING SHOWDOWN

Chiun, reigning Master of Sinanju, looked with horror at what Kali was doing to the hideous remains of what once was Remo.

"Though you are Kali the Terrible and I but an old man," Chiun warned, "I will expend the last of my essence before I allow you to despoil my son's body further."

Kali laughed mockingly, "You are but a mortal husk, bereft of virility, devoid of power. I will gnaw the living flesh from your old bones if you do not begone."

"Bare your teeth then, harlot," said Chiun.

"I hunger for blood," Kali said.

"And I for vengeance," said the Master of Chiun.

*It was the supreme face-off between good and evil. The trouble was, evil had the arms to win. . . .*

# The Destroyer

#86

## ARABIAN NIGHTMARE

Created by
WARREN MURPHY & RICHARD SAPIR

A SIGNET BOOK

SIGNET
Published by the Penguin Group
Penguin Books USA Inc., 375 Hudson Street,
New York, New York 10014, U.S.A.
Penguin Books Ltd, 27 Wrights Lane,
London W8 5TZ, England
Penguin Books Australia Ltd, Ringwood,
Victoria, Australia
Penguin Books Canada Ltd, 10 Alcorn Ave., Suite 300,
Toronto, Canada M4V 3B2
Penguin Books (N.Z.) Ltd, 182–190 Wairau Road,
Auckland 10, New Zealand

Penguin Books Ltd, Registered Offices:
Harmondsworth, Middlesex, England

First published by Signet, an imprint of New American Library, a division of Penguin Books USA Inc.

First Printing, October, 1991
10 9 8 7 6 5 4 3 2 1

PRINTED IN THE UNITED STATES OF AMERICA



PUBLISHER'S NOTE
This is a work of fiction. Names, characters, places, and incidents either are the product of the author's imagination or are used fictitiously, and any resemblance to actual persons, living or dead, events, or locales is entirely coincidental.

Dedicated to all U.S. service personnel who participated in the liberation of Kuwait.

And to the Glorious House of Sinanju, P.O. Box 2505, Quincy, MA 02269.

# 1

The entire world knew that Maddas Hinsein was dead.

They had seen with their own eyes the Tyrant of Irait, the sacker of peaceful Kuran and self-styled Scimitar of the Arabs, being assassinated under the gigantic crossed scimitars of Arab Renaissance Square in downtown Abominadad.

CNN had picked up the Iraiti Information Ministry news feeds. The Iraiti government was determined to show the anti-Irait coalition—particularly the United States—that it did not fear their armies and sanctions. Moreover, it would not allow the murder of its ambassador to the U.S. to go unpunished. The late Turqi Abaatira had been shipped back to Abominadad in an aluminum coffin, the victim of a car accident, according to an apologetic U.S. State Department, which had reluctantly surrendered the remains.

But when President Maddas Hinsein himself had flung open the coffin to see the ambassador's empurpled face, his blackened tongue draped over his chin, and a yellow silk scarf—the symbol of the American human-shield hostages—knotted tightly around his strangled throat, Maddas Hinsein had ordered two of the most prominent of the so-called "guests under duress" to be publicly executed before the world.

The instrument of this dangerous order was no less

than an American agent who had infiltrated Ambominadad to assassinate him. A dead-eyed man with strangely thick wrists who was alleged to answer directly to the U.S. President, but who had fallen under the spell of an American blond named Kimberly Baynes—just as President Hinsein had.

If it were not for the mystical hold this strange young woman had held over Maddas himself, the Scimitar of the Arabs never would have dared order the death of BCN news anchor Don Cooder and perennial presidential candidate turned talk-show host Reverend Juniper Jackman. For Maddas Hinsein had no appetite for war. Only Kuran and its oil wealth.

But he was a proud Arab who had painted himself into the mother of all corners. Since the criminal West had dared murder his ambassador, he was forced to respond in kind, or lose face before his fellow Arabs. He never dreamed that the true murderer was the girl, Kimberly.

Kimberly Baynes had stood off to one side as the doomed Americans were brought up to the wooden gallows steps. She fluttered about in the shapeless black *abayuh* and veil that concealed not only her honeyed hair but also the true focus of Maddas Hinsein's ardor—her four extremely adept arms. They were quite skilled in the spanking arts, to which the Scimitar of the Arabs was partial.

No noose hung from the gallows. Instead, it was choked with Iraiti dignitaries. Most of them men, and all wearing mustaches identical to Maddas' own. They might have been posing for a family-reunion portrait. There were only two *abayuh*-clad women permitted on the platform, and no one knew the identity of the second one—not even Kimberly Baynes.

The moment came. Don Cooder and Reverend Jackman were stood before their executioner. Behind them stood a towering bull of an Arab with soulful eyes and a smile like a sick sun. He wore a green burnoose.

Then the American assassin launched an empty-handed death blow at Don Cooder. In the blink of an eye Kimberly Baynes abruptly snatched the victim from destruction. The only path left for the blow to travel was toward the hapless man in the green burnoose, who happened to stand directly behind the anchorman.

The big mustached man whom the world believed was Maddas Hinsein.

He was jolted backward. The whole world saw it—thanks to the technological miracle of instantaneous satellite transmission.

The President of the United States, one hand on the telephone that would transmit to the Pentagon the order to unleash on Irait the mightiest orchestra of land, sea, and air power assembled in human history, saw the man in the green burnoose catapulted backward as if slammed by a cannonball.

Dr. Harold W. Smith, who in his capacity as director of CURE had ordered the unknown assassin into the Middle East, had heard the distinct thump as the body landed several feet away, under the shadow of the crossed scimitars.

Chiun, the Master of Sinanju, who had trained the nameless assassin, saw his pupil's stunned face as his intended victim was flicked out of the way of the deadly floater stroke. Then one of the *abayuh*-clad women rent her garment apart, exposing white skin, four arms, and a head that canted to one side like a snapped sunflower.

And Sky Bluel, expatriate American peace activist, saw her chance to become the Jane Fonda of the nineties melt away like so much soggy tofu. She already had her Air Irait ticket.

Kimberly Baynes was snapping a yellow scarf between two of her hands. It looped over the assassin's neck, breaking it with an audible snap that was replicated in millions of households worldwide.

The two faced each other, their broken necks tilting in

opposite directions. And their voices made millions of hands reach for volume-control knobs.

*"I am created Shiva the Destroyer; Death, the shatterer of worlds! Who is this dog meat who stands before me?"* So howled the assassin.

*"I am Kali the Terrible; the devourer of life!"* screamed a voice no one could possibly recognize as belonging to Kimberly Baynes. *"And I claim this dance!"*

Howling, they began to drum their feet in unison.

Then pandemonium broke loose. The reviewing stand collapsed in a splintering ruin. The upset cameras veered in every direction, capturing running, panicked feet, blue sky, and one of the Brobdingnagian steel scimitars as it came crashing free of the huge bronze forearm that held it aloft.

Then the satellite feed went black.

No one outside of Abominadad knew what had happened after that. No one knew the fate of Don Cooder or Reverend Jackman, or of the hundreds of U.S. hostages still held at strategic locations throughout Irait. The world held its breath as it wondered what would be the President's response to this latest Iraiti outrage.

But of one thing everyone was certain.

President Maddas Hinsein was no more.

# 2

"His name is Remo," Dr. Harold W. Smith said into the dialless cherry-red telephone.

"Better refer to him as the Caucasian," returned the President of the United States in a cautious voice. "No telling who might be listening in."

"Mr. President," Harold Smith said in a lemony voice, "I assure you this line is absolutely secure. Absolutely."

"Back to the matter at hand," the President said, still guarded. Smith imagined him in the Lincoln Bedroom, where the dedicated line that connected the White House to Folcroft Sanitarium, the headquarters for CURE, was kept in a nightstand drawer. The tension came across the wire like electricity.

"Sir," Harold Smith said wearily, "I watched the same tape you did. It seemed to me that Remo—"

"The Caucasian."

"Our . . . ah . . . operative assassinated Maddas Hinsein."

The President's voice perked up. "Does that mean he was a double agent? I mean, that he wasn't a double agent? It looked for a while that he had become Maddas' personal assassin. His face was on all those threatening Iraiti broadcasts."

"Mr. President, I regret I cannot read into the situation any more than I have. We know that Remo apparently fell under Iraiti control shortly after he went over there."

The President asked, "How is that possible, anyway? He was our best hope of averting war."

"I can offer no opinion on that score," said Harold Smith stiffly. What could he tell the President? That Remo Williams, the human superweapon who for two decades had safeguarded America's shores, had all along been, in reality, the unsuspecting avatar for Shiva, the Hindu god of destruction? That he had fallen under the sway of Kimberly Baynes, a thirteen-year-old girl who had somehow blossomed into a mature woman with four arms, and who might now be Remo's counterpart, the human vessel of the goddess of death, Kali?

No, Harold Smith was not going to volunteer that himself. He could hardly believe it. How could he expect the President, who shared his own salt-of-the-earth New England roots, to accept such a fantasy?

Instead he said, "The problem before you, Mr. President, is determining your best course of action in the aftermath of Hinsein's death."

"I was mentally preparing myself to launch an all-out attack if Abominadad went ahead with a public execution," the President said slowly. 'But without knowing if Cooder and Jackman are dead too, I can't jeopardize our other human-shield hostages over there. The way it looks to the world, the guy the Iraitis have claimed is a renegade U.S. agent turned around and clobbered their leader. That makes us the bad guys. It's a mess."

"The question is, what will Hinsein's war council do?" mused Harold Smith. "Will they agree to withdraw from Kuran, blaming it all on a misadventure engineered by their maverick president, or will they willingly carry out his deadfall commands?"

"That's the part that scares me up a tree," the Commander in Chief admitted ruefully. "If he did leave behind deadfall commands, what were they? To launch terrorist attacks on U.S. targets? To attack our troops in Hamidi Arabia? To gas Israel?"

"Knowing Maddas Hinsein," Harold Smith said soberly, "all three."

"If only we could get a fix on the thinking in Abominadad."

Smith cleared his throat before saying, "Perhaps we can."

"How? Both your people are out of commission. The old Oriental is dead and the Caucasian is missing in action. Our only assets over there are the hostages."

"Correction. The Master of Sinanju is, contrary to earlier reports, alive."

"What?" The President's modified New England accent went south and acquired a startled Texas twang.

"He is recuperating from his coma," Smith added quickly.

"What coma? I understood he was nuked out by Palm Springs."

Smith swallowed uncomfortably, his Adam's apple bobbing out of sight. "If you recall, Mr. President, the situation was this: a jury-rigged neutron bomb had been programmed to detonate in Palm Springs. Remo and Chiun—"

"The Caucasian and the Oriental," the President said quickly.

"—were rushing the neutron device out into the desert to save the population. Time ran out. The . . . um . . . Oriental took the weapon from the other man. The neutron device detonated. There was no trace of the Asian found after the radiation abated."

"Then how—?"

"You'll remember that this matter had to do with a real-estate swindle involving weapons of mass destruction. Near the detonation site was the underground condominium development that was at the heart of the entire matter."

"The Condome, yeah." Smith could visualize his President nodding thoughtfully. It was the President who had helped prepare the cover story that explained away the detonation of a nuclear device in the California desert as an Atomic Energy Commission snafu. Through his society contacts, he had arranged with the parents of the student physicist who had built the device to quietly leave the country. And so Sky Bluel was packed off to finish school in Paris.

Smith went on. "Apparently the Master of Sinanju, knowing that this development had accumulated standing water on its lower floors, dropped the neutron device just before it detonated and found shelter in the flooded floors almost two hundred feet below ground. The combination of sand and water shielded him from the worst of the neutron bombardment."

"Amazing."

"I . . . er . . . suspected that he had survived, and rescued him. He is quite ill, but may recover."

"But he's been presumed dead for months. What on earth tipped you off, Smith?"

Harold Smith hesitated. Could he tell the President that the Spirit of Chiun, Master of Sinanju, had haunted his pupil, Remo, and Smith himself, silently pleading to be rescued from his sandy tomb, until Smith had had the site excavated by the Army Corps of Engineers?

No, Smith decided. He could not tell that to the President. As the head of the supersecret organization that officially did not exist, he was entrusted with one of the nation's most sensitive positions. Telling the truth would put him in the category they used to call Section Eight back in his OSS days.

"I have always been troubled by the lack of a body, Mr. President," he said at last, his vocal cords quivering slightly under the weight of the distasteful lie. "It simply did not occur to me to investigate the Condome site, because it had been sealed with concrete in the immediate aftermath of the detonation."

"I see," mused the President, who was the only man to whom Smith was accountable. "Very good, Smith. The President who selected you for the post you now hold had good judgment—for a Democrat. Too bad they cut him down before he even finished his term."

Smith sighed inwardly. That had been a long time ago. Before Remo. Before Chiun. Before everything.

"It may be that the Master of Sinanju might be able to help us in some way," he went on. "His ancestors—the early Masters of Sinanju—had extensive experience in that part of the world. I will look in on him when we are through discussing the situation."

"Let me know, Smith. I'm going to hold off on a decision until I confer with the other coalition members. I just wanted to check with you first."

"I will be in touch, Mr. President," said Harold Smith, replacing the cherry-red receiver. He then gave his cracked leather executive chair a turn. Rarely oiled ball bearings squealed and grumbled until he found himself facing a plate-glass window of one-way glass and a panoramic view of Long Island Sound and the colorful sails of summer in America.

Dusk was not long off. Summer was on the wane. It seemed, even as he looked out upon the peaceful waters off Rye, New York, where sails luffed and unseen keels etched unreadable signatures on the clear blue slate of water, as if the world was holding its breath.

A vast multinational army stood poised on the border of friendly Hamidi Arabia and occupied Kuran. To the north of that stripped and conquered land, the outlaw nation of Irait, hemmed in by unfriendly powers, isolated by scores of UN resolutions and sanctions, sat like a nuclear core about to go critical from the mounting pressure.

The coalition arrayed against Irait was too fragile to

hold for long, Smith understood. The Germans, Chinese, and Jordanians were secretly dealing in munitions and circumventing that supposedly ironclad blockade. The French were showing signs of collaboration. The Hamidis were growing nervous. Worse, the Syrians were putting out feelers to Abominadad that they might entertain switching sides if the U.S. went on the attack.

And the biggest wild card of all, the Israelis, were dusting off their Jericho missiles for a preemptive strike. No one could blame them, but once Irait unleashed its awesome arsenal of mass destruction, civilization might not be able to pick up the pieces for a thousand years.

Harold Smith removed his rimless glasses and brushed tiny dust motes from the immaculate lenses. He had noticed that in his advancing age these tiny things bothered his weak eyes. Too many long hours hunched over a computer screen—scanning his vast data bank for incipient danger signals, guarding the nation from the forces that would twist the Constitution against the land that had birthed it—had made his gray eyes hypersensitive.

A freak of glancing light made the glass window dimly reflective. Smith stared at his own pinched, lemony features, took in the grayed hair that was only a shade or two lighter than his three-piece suit, and understood that the world was poised at a crossroad in history. If all went well, a new world order would emerge in the coming decade. If not, a new Dark Ages loomed. CURE would be needed more than ever—and he was an old man with failing eyes and no enforcement arm.

Smith gave the lenses a final brush, replaced them, and heaved his lanky Ichabod Crane body out of the chair.

He strode wordlessly past his busy secretary and took the elevator to the third floor.

The Master of Sinanju was in the sanitarium's private wing.

Smith knocked politely on the door.

A cracked and querulous voice said, "Enter, O Emperor."

Smith suppressed a start. When he had last looked in on the Master of Sinanju, he was a sunken shell, seemingly clinging to life by the thinnest of threads.

Yet through the heavy oak door Chiun had recognized Smith, whom he called emperor because in the five-thousand-year history of the House of Sinanju, no Master had ever served one who was not royalty—except in disgrace. And Chiun, the reigning Sinanju master of this century, refused to acknowledge that he was any less great than his predecessors.

Thus Smith was Emperor Smith, sometimes Harold the Generous. Other times, Mad Harold. He bore it in stoic distaste, because if there was one thing he had learned since the day he had hired Chiun to train a Newark beat cop named Remo Williams to become CURE's enforcement arm, it was not to directly disagree with the Master of Sinanju.

Clearing his throat, Smith opened the door and stepped in.

Chiun lay under the white sheets, his birdlike head resting on the pillow. No muscle seemed to move on his frail exposed arms. Only the eyes, as hazel as mahogany buttons, showed life. They flicked in Smith's direction.

"How are you feeling, Master Chiun?" Smith asked as he approached the bed.

"As well as can be expected," said Chiun, putting a dry rattle in his voice that had not been there before.

Catching the prompt, Smith played along.

"Is there somethig wrong?"

"The nurses are brutes," Chiun croaked. "Except for the one who personally prepares my rice. She should be allowed to live."

"It is against Folcroft policy to execute the nurses on the basis of poor performance," Smith said soberly.

"I would accept a caning, if it were severe enough."

"Corporal punishment is out of the question. But if you are insistent, I can have them terminated—I mean let go," Smith added hastily.

The Master of Sinanju closed his eyes wearily. "Yes, by all means let them go. Over a precipice."

Smith examined Chiun's head with a sinking feeling of despair. The puffs of hair over each seashell ear seemed dull and gray, the wisp of a beard that curled from his chin thin and insubstantial as incense. The aged face, like an amber raisin, was a network of radiating wrinkles, the closed eyes sunk in their bony orbits as if receding into death and corruption.

Perhaps it was that the Master of Sinanju was still recovering from his months of coma suspended in a dark body of stagnant water like an insect larva. Possibly it was because Smith had only recently learned that Chiun had turned one hundred, but the old Korean seemed far, far older than before. He looked helpless beyond words, in fact. Smith despaired of the future of the organization he helmed.

"The nurses told me you watched the transmission from Abominadad," Smith said carefully.

No response.

"You saw what happened to Remo."

Chiun's papery lips thinned in a bloodless line.

Smith pressed on. "Do you think that Remo can be salvaged?"

The pause was long before the answer came. "No."

"Does that mean you would not undertake such a task?"

"I am an old man, and very ill. The task before me is to become well. There is no other objective possible. Or desirable."

"It was not Remo's fault that he did not understand your . . . appearances."

"*You* understood," Chiun said disapprovingly.

"I was not as emotionally involved as Remo," Harold

Smith explained. "He interpreted your repeated gesture of pointing to the ground as indicating his feet. He thought you were trying to tell him that he walked in your sandals now."

"My spirit appeared to him four times," Chiun intoned. "He did not understand because he did not want to understand. He covets my title. I have given up my retirement years to train a pale piece of pig's ear, and when I needed him most, he pretended to be a tree ape and scratched his head in puzzlement."

He turned his wizened face to the wall.

Smith decided to change his approach.

"I have just been on the telephone with the President of the United States."

"Hail to the chief," Chiun muttered.

"He was wondering what insights you might have," Smith went on. "Your ancestors worked for the Iraitis when they were the Mesopotamians."

"Bong worked for them. Bong the Worthless. He had alienated the Persians and the Egyptians, and was forced to make do with inferior clients."

"Ahem. They are entrenching themselves in occupied Kuran."

"Worms also dig holes."

"They refuse to knuckle under in the face of overwhelming economic ruin."

"They have always been poor. How much poorer can they become? It is all the same to those barbarians."

Smith listened to the bitterness of the old Korean's voice. He understood it. The Masters of Sinanju had always shouldered a cruel burden, hiring themselves out as assassins and protectors to the thrones of antiquity, because the village of Sinanju, situated on the bleak rocky shores of modern North Korea, could not support itself through fishing or industry. In the bad years, they drowned the children. It was called "sending the babies home to the sea."

Over the centuries, the House of Sinanju had risen in power and influence. The Masters of Sinanju learned every killing art there was, perfected many new ones, and then in the days of the Great Wang transcended the so-called martial arts when Wang discovered the sun source—the inner power that enabled the Masters of Sinanju to overcome human limitations and frailties to fully realize the potential of their minds and bodies.

More feared than the ninjas, more hated that the Borgias, more powerful than an army of Visigoths on the march, the Masters of Sinanju rose up from the mud flats of an inhospitable village to stand supreme in the martial arts.

A long line, proud, haughty, unbroken. Until the time of Chiun, whose original Korean pupil went renegade, leaving him with no replacement until America had asked him to do an impossible, unforgivable thing—train a white man in the forbidden art of Sinanju.

The last of his line, Chiun had done this thing. And in the long years that followed, he had discovered that Remo Williams possessed the promise of greatness. Chiun dared to dream that Remo was the fulfillment of a half-forgotten legend of Sinanju that foretold the coming of a dead night tiger who would be the avatar of Shiva the Destroyer, and would ultimately become the greatest Master of them all.

Remo was. And had. But Remo had become increasingly subject to personality transformations, in which the spirit of Shiva had peered through Remo's mortal eyes.

Now, at the worst possible time, Remo had become Shiva. Chiun had seen this on television. Kimberly Baynes had broken his neck, liberating the spirit of Shiva. Remo was no more.

It meant that the Sinanju line ended with Chiun. In fulfilling the prophecy, Chiun had abolished the very thing he had sacrificed so much to perpetuate.

Worse, Chiun had come to love Remo like a son. Now

he felt abandoned and betrayed. Life held no more sweetness for him.

Harold Smith adjusted his striped Dartmouth tie. He smoothed it down absently. Neither gesture was needed.

"I understand how you feel," he said carefully.

Chiun looked up with interest. "You have a son?"

"A daughter."

His eyes became slits of cold light. "Then you do not understand."

"The President is uncertain whether or not he should order a strike against Abominadad."

"Strike them," Chiun said flatly. "The world will be better off."

"It would be a devastating strike. Remo would undoubtedly perish."

Chiun waved a dismissive hand. "Remo is no more. Shiva walks in his shoes. Your President could no more obliterate Shiva than a Master of Sinanju could pull down the moon with a net of spiderwebs. Inform him he should not wait."

Smith's stooped shoulders visibly sagged. "Then I guess you will be returning to Sinanju."

"There is time. My contract has not yet expired. I will fulfill that—within the limitations that my long ordeal has inflicted on me."

"I am sorry to inform you, Master Chiun," Harold Smith said, thinking quickly, "but your contract expired several weeks ago."

Chiun's eyes snapped open in fright. A faint electrical sensation came into the room. It was coming from Chiun.

"Truly?" he squeaked, his voice vibrating like a plucked harp string.

"Truly."

"This is terrible."

"I might consider an extension."

"I do not mean that," Chiun flared. "I mean that I have missed my *kohi.*"

Smith blinked. "Excuse me?"

"It is a Korean word," Chiun explained. "It means 'old and rare.' When a Master of Sinanju reaches his one hundredth birthday, he is said to have achieved his *kohi*. It is a time of great celebration. And I am the first Master of Sinanju to miss his *kohi* for reasons other than death." He heaved a tiny sigh. "Truly, I am cursed by the gods."

"I am sorry to hear that," Smith said tonelessly.

"Leave me now. I am disconsolate."

"Of course."

Smith moved toward the door. The Master of Sinanju's eyes slowly closed. The faint electricity in the air began subsiding.

At the door, Smith paused.

"By the way," he said, "have you insurance?"

Chiun's voice was distant. "Why do you ask?"

"Well, the sanitarium charges over three hundred dollars a day," Smith explained. "The private nurses are extra, of course. And the television is twenty-five dollars a day. To whom shall I send the bill?"

Chiun sat up like a switchblade folding.

"Bill!" he squeaked. "I have served your organization for two miserable decades! And you demand repayment?"

"I must. This is Folcroft, not the organization. Technically, they are separate operating budgets. I cannot forgive the debt of one on behalf of the other."

Chiun's eyes went narrow and steely.

"You have saved me, Harold Smith, from a cold eternity of emptiness," he began.

"I appreciate your gratitude," Smith said levelly.

"I am not grateful," Chiun said coldly, "for I have returned to bitterness and ingratitude on all sides. Better that you had left me to bob like a dried apricot in the eternal Void than return me to such gracelessness."

"Perhaps we might work something out," Smith suggested.

Chiun's eyes squeezed into bitter blades.

"How?"

"I could forgive the debt, in return for your consulation on the Iraiti situation."

Chiun's eyes squeezed tighter. But for a lean, menacing glitter, they might have been closed.

"Is that not mixing your businesses?" he demanded.

"CURE can legally pay you a consulting fee, out of which you may repay Folcroft for your medical expenses."

"No," Chiun said in a firm voice.

"No?"

"I must have double," said Chiun, his voice rising anew. "Double because I have endured the tortures of nurses who should be working in mines deep underground rather than attending one such as I."

"I would agree to that," Smith said coolly.

"Good. I must have several items from you, Smith."

"Name them."

"A brazier, the shell of a leopard tortoise, and the exact birth hour of Maddas Hinsein."

Harold Smith's gray eyebrows lifted in surprise. "Why do you need Hinsein's birthdate?"

"Because he is not dead," said Chiun, slipping back onto his pillow.

# 3

Maddas Hinsein ran for his life from the baroque expanse of Arab Renaissance Square.

He was not alone. It seemed as if all of Abominadad were fleeing the square and the fury that had unleashed itself upon the world.

Twin furies, actually.

Maddas, tripping over the hem of his *abayuh*, craned his veiled face around to once again behold the terrible sight.

What his morose brown eyes saw filled him with a great dread.

The gallows that had been converted into a reviewing stand was now a shipwreck of splinters and rude boards. More frightening, one of the giant bronze forearms—cast from a mold of Maddas' own—had cracked asunder. The scimitar one huge fist clutched was balanced in the puny human-sized hands of the assassin who now wielded it as if it were a mere plastic swizzle stick instead of the ponderous product of the finest German swordsmiths.

It pointed straight upward, balanced, teetering. The blade began to descend. It *swooshed* like a jet taking off.

Under the blade stood Kimberly Baynes, nude, her broken neck tilted to one side, her eyes, once limpid pools of violet ink, now burning like balls of phosphorescent blood in an angry face that Maddas barely recognized.

They went wide as exploding suns as, hissing, the blade chopped down.

The ground shook. Sparks spit from the cracking concrete like a devil's anvil being worked. The blade rang like the mighty sword of Allah smiting the infidel.

And floating out from the vibration, a musical voice rang, mocking, insolent.

*"Come, Shiva. This is no way to treat your bride!"*

It was the voice of sweet Kimberly Baynes, and yet it was not.

She stood off to one side, her four arms lifting like a spider preparing to pounce upon its prey. Her small breasts shook.

The blade lifted again. It described a figure eight in the air, the flutter and swish of the fine blade impossibly loud as it cleaved the air.

This time it came in sideways, seeking her smooth neck.

Nimble and light-footed, Kimberly leapt to avoid it. The terrible edge whizzed under her. She alighted on all six limbs like a sinister sleek insect sheathed in human flesh.

*"Lay down your sword, O Shiva,"* Kimberly proclaimed. *"Kali claims you now. We will dance the Tandava and this land shall become the Caldron of Blood from which we shall both quaff mightily."*

The answer was an inhuman roar, loud, terrible, deafening.

It came from a man who wore a scarlet-and-purple costume that evoked images of genies, harems, and the *Arabian Nights*. His skin was a raw sunburned tone and his eyes burned like coals aflame. His thick-wristed hand balanced the other scimitar like a red ant carrying a twig.

The blade crashed down again. Kimberly dodged expertly.

This time it struck a prostrate figure in a green burnoose, chopping it in two. The separate parts of the body jumped into the sky.

The sight of his official spokesman, Selim Fanek—whom Maddas Hinsein had wisely arranged to take his place on the gallows—flying upward in two sections reminded the Scimitar of the Arabs of how this gold-haired vixen had betrayed him. Were it not for his own cunning, Maddas himself would now be flying skyward in pieces like so much cordwood. It was Fanek who had taken the traitorous fatal blow meant for Maddas himself.

He turned and resumed his run, a hulking figure in his feminine *abayuh* and black paratroop boots. He had to find sanctuary in this madness of betrayal. For soon the deadfall commands he had left with his trusted defense minister would be executed.

And he knew also that soon the American bombs would fall. Maddas Hinsein could live with the downfall of his people. But he, too, was on ground zero. And the Scimitar of the Arabs had a greater destiny to fulfill than becoming so much mulch. One that did not include ignominious death.

He had to find sanctuary.

A man stumbled across his path. He was an old one, with but a single yellow-brown tooth in his head.

"Allah forgive us!" the elder moaned. "For the sins of our wicked leader, we have been sent two demons to bedevil us."

"Curse you, old man!" snapped Maddas Hinsein, stomping out the pitiful man's lone tooth with the heel of a boot. "You are too weak to enjoy the triumph that lies before the Iraiti people."

Maddas plunged on, melting into the fleeing crowd.

* * *

Elsewhere in Abominadad, two frightened men were being carried along with the human wave escaping the carnage of Arab Renaissance Square.

"Can you see what's happening back there?" huffed Don Cooder, hostage anchor for the American television network BCN. His hair actually stood up on end—the result of a lifetime of hair-spray abuse.

"No," puffed Reverend Juniper Jackman, who had come to Abominadad to upstage and liberate Cooder, only to end up his cellmate. "Why should I care? Gettin' out alive's all that matters."

"We just witnessed a turning point in history," Cooder went on, his voice taking on a stentorian timbre. "Maddas, the Tyrant of Irait, has suffered the same overreaching fate as previous Iraiti despots. Someone has to inform the world."

"If I spot a phone booth," Reverend Jackman said distractedly, "I'll let you know."

"I'd give anything for a four-wire line at this crucial, pivotal, important moment in history I have been privileged to witness."

"And I'd give anything if someone would just beam me back to Washington. As a famous man said once, 'Fame is fleeting, but my ass is forever.' "

The crowd was scurrying like ragged lemmings for a cliff. Don Cooder and the Reverend Jackman were carried along by fear and the threat of trampling feet. If they tripped or stumbled, they would be instantly stomped into bloody rags. The thought of the closed-coffin funerals that would result made their blood run cold. Neither of them had come to Abominadad to be denied a last moment in the limelight—even if it was while lying amid black crepe and purple velvet.

As the stampede of men, women, and children flooded into the city proper, it was forced into a channel made by two lines of office buildings.

"Think they'll ever stop?" Cooder gasped.

"Up with hope," Jackman wheezed.

A cold, blocky building suddenly appeared in the path of the human flood. It almost blocked the other end of the street.

The crowd attempted to go around it. But the momentum of their flight was too great, the multitude pressed too closely, for most to manage.

"Oh, shoot," Reverned Jackman moaned.

Part of the leading edge of the crowd actually smashed into the squat building like starlings into a 747's intakes. They made quite an ugly sound as they began piling up.

The more nimble members of this surging clot of fleeing humanity thinned, and broke in two directions.

Suddenly the way before Don Cooder and Reverend Jackman parted like the Red Sea. They saw the slumping bodies.

And they saw the limestone facade, a bulwark of bodies crushed before it, seemingly coming at them.

"I'm gonna die in a heathen land!" Reverend Jackman yelped.

"I'm gonna die," Don Cooder moaned, "and there's no one to film my tragic yet ironic conclusion."

Jackman turned around, eyes sick, anxious, as if a camera might somehow materialize to preserve their last heroic moments on earth.

Then he noticed it.

"Hey, showboat, wait up!" he yelled.

"Are you crazy? I'll be trampled."

"No, you won't," said Reverend Jackman, his voice suddenly far away.

Cooder's head snapped back, thinking Jackman had fallen under the remorseless feet of the crowd.

But when he looked back, he saw Reverend Juniper Jackman bent over, chest working like a bellows, retching as he tried to get his wind back.

The stampede that had been hot on their heels had

veered away in both directions to avoid the squat building.

Realization dawned on Don Cooder. That meant he could stop too.

He no sooner signaled his brain to slide into a skid than the side of his head slammed limestone and he joined the pile of slumped Iraiti bodies.

"You dead?" Reverend Jackman asked after he had regained his breath and sidled up.

"Is my face still photogenic?" Cooder asked, clutching his head.

"No. Never was."

Cooder closed his eyes. "Then I'm dead."

"For a hick Texan with bags under his eyes clear down to his belly button, you make a lively noise, though," Reverend Jackman added.

"Then I won't ask you to put me out of my misery," Don Cooder said, sitting up.

'You won't have to. I'll bet any amount of money that folks think we're dead already."

Don Cooder's glowing black eyes lit up.

"Think of our triumphant return to the States: 'Hostage anchor and irrelevant black politician turned talk-show host return from the dead.' "

"Hey, cut that 'irrelevant' part out, hear? I'm shadow senator of the District of Columbus now."

"It's District of Columbia, and if they break programming when they get the glad news, it'll be on account of me, not you."

"Let 'em," Reverend Jackman muttered, looking up to the sky. "I just don't want to be dead for real. 'Cause if my people hear I'm a goner, they're gonna insist the President bomb the pooh out of this heckhole in retaliation."

"We must find shelter!" Don Cooder's head jerked this way and that. "Do you see anything? Anything that looks substantial?"

"Nothing," Jackman said airily. "Unless you count this fine upstanding building you slammed into."

Cooder's eyes came into focus then. "Oh. Yeah," he said weakly. "That."

Jackman helped the anchor to his feet.

"You are one hell of a reporter, you know that?" Jackman growled. "You run smack into probably the best bomb shelter in town and you don't have sense enough to notice."

"Even Cronkite would be rattled after what happened to us," Cooder said, straightening his wrinkled suit. With a grandiose gesture he flung the door open. Then, recalling where he was, he executed a sudden reversal, saying, "Ministers before anchormen."

Cautiously Reverend Jackman crept in. Cooder counted to ten using his fingers. When he heard no gunshots, he followed.

The place was dark. The electricity was off. The signs were in Arabic so it was impossible to tell what purpose the building served.

"What *did* happen to us?" Jackman asked. "It came and went so fast, it was kind of a blur."

"That guy with the dead eyes was fixing to kill us," said Cooder.

"Yeah. The white guy with the wrists like two-by-fours. He looked like an American, except he was dressed like outta the *Arabian Nights*. He was gonna do us barehanded, too. I remember him saying he was sorry he had to do it."

They started up the stairs.

"That was to you," Don Cooder said. "To me he said my murder was going to be a pleasure."

Jackman grunted. "Musta been a right-winger. They all got it in for you."

"No, he seemed to know me from somewhere. And he looked kinda familiar, to boot. He said something else. But I think it was knocked out of me."

"Not the first time," Jackman grunted.

They climbed five flights before they gave it up and started going room to room, trying telephones. All were dead. Not that it mattered much. They were in enemy territory, and condemned to die by Maddas Hinsein's Revolting Command Council. Even it they knew the Iraiti equivalent of 911, it probably wouldn't help.

They found a window that faced toward the broad plaza of Arab Renaissance Square.

"Maybe we can see something from here," Jackman suggested.

The square was virtually deserted. The crossed scimitars that had pierced the sumptuous skyline still did, they were surprised to see. In fact, they were still crossed.

A harsh clang greeted their ears. Even through the sealed window, it made their teeth rattle in sympathy.

"Ouch, that hurt," Cooder said uneasily. The twin blades vibrated so much the phenomenon was visible even from their distant vantage point.

Then the blades unlocked, stood apart momentarily, and came at one another with renewed fury. The pane of glass broke before their eyes, so great was the shock wave that rippled from the clashing blades.

"They're not supposed to move!" Don Cooder blurted. "They're monuments."

"Well, they're moving now," said Reverend Juniper Jackman, licking his scraggly mustache in worriment. His pop eyes seemed to stick out further than usual. He had the furtive look of a compulsive arsonist who, upon awakening from a bender, smelled gasoline on his fingertips and couldn't recall how it got there.

Don Cooder drew in his breath. "What could be causing this? What incredible power, unseen, unknowable, unstoppable—?"

"I'm gonna unstop you if you don't stop talking like you're reading the seven-o'clock lead," Reverend Jackman spat. "Where do you get that stuff, anyway?"

Cooder shrugged. "All our news writers come over from the *Enquirer*. Saves us breaking them in."

"Figures."

Their eyes returned to the glass. The scimitars were in motion again. Once more the glass popped, the air reverberating with a metallic clang and crash. The sparks that leapt from the joined blades were as big as snowballs.

"You know," said Reverend Juniper Jackman, "I can't see what's got hold of those pigstickers, but I got me a notion it has something to do with that guy who tried to off us."

Don Cooder nodded. "I wasn't gonna bring this up, but just before everything came crashing down around us, did you happen to notice an Arab gal rip her clothes clean off?"

"Maybe," Reverend Jackman said hesitantly.

"Did you notice her arms?"

"Arms? Yeah, I noticed arms. A few."

"How many did you count?"

"I stopped at three," admitted Reverend Jackman. "Three arms on a woman is unchristian. I didn't wanna see no more."

"I counted four," muttered Don Cooder in a thin voice.

Silence fell in the dim room. Neither man had anything to add to that shared recollection.

A scimitar longer than a jet's wing twisted and slashed across the skyline. Its opponent blade drew back, avoiding the blow. The attacking blade continued uninterrupted.

It bit into the side of a building like a knife through cardboard. The building's facade abruptly collapsed. It was a cheap concrete apartment building, but still the concrete should not have crumbled so easily. The blow must have been terrific.

So must the backswing have been. It chopped a line of flagpoles, on which the Iraiti national flag fluttered in triplicate, clean in two.

"I figure the gal has the other blade," Reverend Jackman said at last. His voice was very small.

"I figure the same," said Don Cooder. "Thing of it is, why are they fightin'?"

"I think the gal broke the guy's neck."

"I thought it was the gal who had a neck that was broken," Cooder countered. "It leaned over to one side like a Texas buzzard eyeing a sick steer."

"Well, they both got broken necks, then. It happens.

The blades swung madly, dancing, emitting flashing rays of bronze and gold sunlight, as they waved and evaded one another.

"Looks like they're getting the hang of it now," Don Cooder said after a while.

Jackman squinted. "Look to you like they're getting closer?"

"Maybe? Why?"

" 'Cause if they are, we're right on the chopping block, I figure."

"When you suppose the bombs will start falling?"

"No tellin'."

"Then I vote we take our chances," said Cooder. "The way they're going at it, all those bombs will be good for is to smooth out the rubble anyway."

Reverend Jackman shook his head stubbornly. "Not me. This hunk of stone looks built to last. I'm stayin' right here until it ain't safe no more."

"If you're staying, then I'm staying," Cooder said, letting his famous granite jaw jut out like the prow on an Aegis cruiser. But his saggy eyes were uneasy.

All at once the glass in front of them simply fell out. And the gargantuan contending blades hadn't even connected.

Reverend Juniper Jackman and Don Cooder jumped back, grabbing one another in fear.

"I'll go if you'll go," Cooder whispered.

"I'll go if goin' stays our little secret," Jackman hissed.

"You won't tell my public?"

"If you don't breathe a word to my constituency."

"Deal, brother."

They bombed down the stairs holding hands like a two frightened children scampering from a haunted house.

Except that the true horrors lurked outside the building, not within it.

# 4

General Razzik Azziz, defense minister of all Irait and occupied Kuran, burst into the headquarters of the Revolting Command Council, out of breath, his eyes sick with fear, and his brown face sheathed in a layer of perspiration deep enough to fry onion rings.

Most of the other council members had already beat him to the room, he was horrified to realize. They sat around the square council table, their identical mustaches twitching and quirking nervously.

To Azziz's profound surprise, none had claimed the seat formerly occupied by the late President Maddas Hinsein.

Sensing the opportunity to seize power by the simple application of his backside to morocco leather, General Razzik Azziz hastily plunked himself down.

He saw no opposition from the others, so his tight features broke into a wide grin under the sweat-dewed mustache.

"I hearby declare myself President for Life, the natural successor of our beloved leader, Maddas the Unforgettable," Azziz said in his most formal voice.

To his astonishment, the Revolting Command Council—or such of them as had survived the apparent coup in Arab Renaissance Square—burst out in relieved applause.

"I further hereby declare that from this day forward,"

he announced, "the decree that all Iraitis must emulate our former Precious Leader in all ways, especially as regards to facial hair, is this instant repealed."

More applause. President Razzik Azziz scowled. This was too easy. What were they up to?

"Henceforth," he added, "I will be addressed as *al-Rais*, the President."

Even more applause. Two men, the iron-haired foreign minister and the prissy-faced minister of information, stood up in a modest standing ovation.

"No," Azziz said suddenly. "*Al-Ze'em*, the Leader."

Everyone stood up now. The applause swelled.

This, President Razzik Azziz knew, was not typical Iraiti behavior in the halls of power. For thousands of years, going back to the empires of ancient Assyria and Babylon, the vestigial roots of modern Irait, the rulers of this land had to murder and torture their way to the top, and as often as not ultimately died by assassination.

Something was very, very wrong.

But, not having any clue as to what that might be, Azziz pushed on, consolidating power.

"Now that this is settled, we must deal with the Kuran problem," he announced as he motioned for the others to take their seats. "An accommodation must be reached with the American forces, who are not responsible for our ambassador's fate, according to secret information I have obtained."

"What about the Palestinian problem?" asked the minister of education.

President Azziz made a face. He turned to the information minister, saying, "Release this statement. 'I, President Razzik Azziz of the Republic of Irait, hereby declare that I will defend the cause of Palestine to the very last drop of Palestinian blood.' "

With that settled, so that no one would doubt his meaning, President Azziz went on: "We must get word to Washington of our intention to return the Arab land of Kuran to the scavengers who had held it. We no longer wish to inhabit it. We have everything of value anyway, including the imported English cobblestones."

"What about the United Nations forces?" the foreign minister asked. "Once we retreat, they will advance into Kuran and establish a base near our true southern border. Then we shall never be rid of them."

"We will never be rid of them as long as they have an excuse to attack," President Azziz said, slapping the table. "Have this done. We will deal with the consequences later."

The foreign minister nodded. "At once."

"Then inform Washington and other capitals that from this moment on, the hostages—"

"Guests under duress," corrected the information minister, who had coined the diplomatic neologism.

"—guests under duress," finished President Azziz, "are free to leave without restriction or hindrance."

"Is that wise?" asked the minister of education.

President Azziz, seeing the beginnings of opposition, considered pulling out his service pistol and shooting the man dead where he sat. But upon reflection, he thought it impolitic to shoot council members in the first ten minutes of his term of office.

Instead he asked, "Why do you ask?"

"The American agents who are even now running amok in Arab Renaissance Square," offered the education minister. "Should you not make their surrender a condition of this gesture toward peace and goodwill?"

This was actually an excellent idea, thought President Azziz, who had momentarily forgotten the terrible sight in the square from which he and the others had fled.

He made a mental note to have the man tried for treason at the earliest pretext that presented itself. He was too smart for his own good. Besides, Azziz had a brother-in-law who would make a perfect education minister. The man could actually read.

"Let this be a condition of our terms," he pronounced.

Just then the cultural minister burst in, hot, sweaty, and thoroughly frightened.

"They are ruining the city!" he shouted. "Why does no one stop them?"

"Because we have no defense minister," replied President Azziz in a reasonable tone.

"But you are the defense minister, Azziz."

Then the cultural minister recognized that Razzik Azziz sat in the Precious Leader's chair.

"You may address me as *al-Ze'em*," said Razzik Azziz, pride causing his mustache to bristle manfully.

"*Al-Ze'em*, they are monsters," the man said quickly. "The woman is possessed by demons and the man roars like Shaitan himself unleashed upon the world. They have taken up the scimitars of Maddas Hinsein himself and are battling as if to end the world!"

"Who is winning?" demanded Azziz.

"I could not say. But Abominadad, it is surely losing. They have leveled the square and are moving this way."

"I promote you to defense minister, my brother, and charge you with the sacred duty of defending our ancient capital from naked aggression."

"The blond woman, her aggression is truly naked. For she wears no *abayuh*. Also, she possesses the limbs of a poisonous spider."

"Then exterminate them both this instant."

The new defense minister hastened away to perform his sacred duty.

President Azziz addressed the others. "I suggest we witness our unavoidable victory from the roof," he said confidently.

From the roof of the Palace of Sorrows they could see, imperfectly and only at intervals, the conflict raging several miles away.

Most often visible were the blades. The tiny figures that wielded them were not at all visible.

The clashing scimitars struck sparks that actually started small fires around the center of battle. Sirens whined. The roads were choked with the fleeing.

The green-onion shape of the Tomb of the Unknown Martyr shook like a ceramic bell as the scimitars clashed and sprang apart directly behind it.

"Can you see them?" asked the President.

"No, *al-Ze'em!*" came the crisp answer. "Only the great blades."

One scimitar twisted and whirled, pushing back at the other. On the backswing, it sliced through the green dome as if it were a simple bowl. The crash and rattle of falling debris made everyone assembled on the roof think of an earthquake.

"There!" said the education minister. "I see one! It is the yellow-haired demoness."

Between two buidings, Kimberly Baynes stepped into view. Her slim body was entirely nude. With each swing, her hair flung about like a horse's tail. The blade—its hilt larger than she—was firmly grasped by four spidery arms.

"She is very strong, even for a woman with four arms," a voice muttered.

"She had come to Greater Araby to sow destruction and flaunt her shameless un-Islamic customs," said President Azziz grimly.

"She is certainly flaunting her customs," said the culture minister turned defense minister, who had joined them. They noticed he was training a pair of field glasses on the scene.

"Are her . . . um . . . customs as large as those of our Arab women?" asked the president.

"No, they are actually quite small, these customs."

The field glasses began to make the rounds. Everyone

wanted a peek at the surprisingly small charms of the American demon from hell.

Then they heard a whirring *whup-whup-whup* sound bouncing between the baroque manmade canyons of Abominadad.

From the north came a trio of Soviet-made Hind gunships. The big helicopters floated over the rooftops, their rotors amazingly quiet for such massive craft. Their desert-colored bodies were heavy with rocket pods and chin-mounted machine guns. They resembled nothing so much as high-tech baked potatoes.

The Hinds came in low, circled the zone of conflict once, and broke off to attack.

"They are doomed now," promised the defense minister.

A pod let go, gushing a string of rockets. They arrowed down toward the broken mosquelike monument, destroying it utterly.

The upraised blades poised in the air like startled moth feelers.

"They missed," said the education minister.

"The defense minister is new at his job," suggested the president, remembering how it had been for him. He had been a mere orderly at the start of the long Irait-Irug war. Twelve previous defense ministers had been executed or perished in "accidents" after displeasing former President Maddas Hinsein. Eventually Azziz had found himself next in line. Since execution came more quickly to those who declined field promotions than to those who angered the president, he had accepted the offer joyfully.

Another Hind made a run at the flashing scimitars.

This one cut loose with its chin-mounted machine gun. It seemed a sensible approach, inasmuch as the rate of fire was capable of felling a small forest. Until the other scimitar—the one not wielded by the nude blond demon—swept across the skyline and simply chopped the tail off the Hind.

It fell in two pieces. After it disappeared behind a baroque toadstool-shaped water tower, a fireball of boiling flame and sooty smoke ascended to the sky from the spot where it had last been seen.

The third Hind withdrew to a respectful distance, where it was quickly joined by the second. They hovered like fat dragonflies, lining up their guns and rocket pods.

"This is excellent," said the defense minister. "They are going to obliterate the demons now."

Evidently the so-called demons realized this too. They ceased their fearsome clash. The scimitars poised momentarily like a cosmic pair of shears.

Then one of them pulled back, paused, and swept out.

It was too far away to strike the menacing gunships, although they wobbled in the sky from the backwash of air.

The scimitar drew back all the way, disappearing from sight.

When it appeared again, it was a spinning disk of metal that flew through the air with an ominous sound like a gigantic bull roarer.

"Impossible!" President Azziz exploded. "He has thrown it!"

Like a giant rotor that had slipped its mast, the scimitar whirled toward the hovering Hinds.

Every member of the Revolting Command Council knew what the result was going to be. Only the defense minister, who saw his career going down in flames on the first day of the job, turned away as the giant scimitar decapitated the poised Hinds of their supporting rotors.

The rotors flew off in two directions, shedding sharp blades that caught the glancing sunlight. One snapped a minaret like a breadstick.

The Hinds dropped like baked potatoes from seared hands and the blast of fire that they surrendered upon impact caused the sweat on every face of the Revolting Command Council to evaporate.

"What should we do?" muttered the defense minister. "The Americans are obviously unstoppable."

"Why do you ask us?" demanded Razzik Azziz. "You are the new defense minister."

"But you are the old one, *al-Ze'em*. You have expertise in these matters. I am only a fortunate culture minister. All I know is torture and espionage. Neither of which applies here."

Razzik Azziz looked out over the smoke and flames peppering the heart of the city. Only one scimitar waved amid the boiling smoke. Oddly, it had grown quiescent, as if the wielder was unwilling to carry on mortal combat with his unarmed opponent.

"I say we immediately release all hostages and surrender unconditionally," Azziz said.

"If you do that," put in the education minister, "the Americans will insist upon war-crimes tribunals and necks to fill out their cruel nooses."

"Then we will surrender the architect of these crimes, our dead Precious Leader," Azziz said.

"But the Americans will insist upon a live neck. What they call a scrape goat."

"Scapegoat," corrected President Razzik Azziz, who was growing impatient with this too-smart education minister. "Whom should we offer them?"

On the roof of the Palace of Sorrows, the eyes of the Revolting Command Council flicked away from the face of their leader. Guilty looks made their expressions strange.

"Answer me!" demanded President Azziz.

It was, of course, the insolent education minister who offered a trembling opinion.

"It is not whom we will offer them, *al-Ze'em*," he said tightly. "It is whom they will insist upon hanging. And with our beloved Maddas in the merciful hands of Allah, you, *al-Ze'em*, are the natural choice."

President Razzik Azziz blinked, a nervous tic crawling

along his mustachioed features. It started at his left eye, worked down diagonally, causing his nostrils to flare, and finally sent his mustache jerking like an inchworm on a hot plate.

Now, too late, he understood. It was all very clear to him. The reason no one else had leapt into the president's chair before him was a simple one. It was no longer the seat of power, but a throne of death.

And he had claimed it for his own.

# 5

Harold Smith was surprised to find the Master of Sinanju seated on a tatami mat at the foot of his hospital bed.

Chiun wore a bone-white kimono which Smith had personally recovered from a steamer trunk in the Master of Sinanju's nearby home. He sat lotus-style, his back arched, his wizened features screwed up in concentration as he inscribed quick black brushstrokes on a parchment scroll. The overhead lights made hot blobs of light on his bald head. A covered wok simmered at his feet.

"The President has received an urgent communication from Abominadad," Smith began.

Without looking up, Chiun nodded.

"The defense minister of Irait has offered to release all hostages if the U.S. will call off the destructive forces they claim we have unleashed upon their city."

Chiun frowned, adding a brushstroke to the geometrical pattern he had been carefully creating on the parchment.

"The trouble is," Smith went on, "we have unleashed nothing. We believe the Iraitis are referring to Remo and Kimberly Baynes."

"This is not good," Chiun said, his frown making his face shrivel into a mummylike death mask. Leaping flames from a tiny Sterno fire sent wavering blue shadows across the Master of Sinanju's dry features like the ghostly turning of the pages of history.

"Are you referring to the fact that we have no control over Remo and Kimberly?"

"No," said Chiun, "I am referring to the fact that your opponent, Maddas Hinsein, was born with the sun in Taurus. This is very bad. It means he is stubborn and intractable. He will not surrender until he is dead. And perhaps not even then."

"How can that be?" Smith wondered.

"For a true Taurus, this is possible."

After dipping a stiff writing stick into an ink stone, the Master of Sinanju made another brushstroke.

"The moon in Scorpio," he added.

"What does that mean?"

"He enjoys dressing as a woman." Chiun looked up, his eyes glinting. "That explains how he still lives."

Smith cleared his throat. "Er, Master Chiun, I must inform you that the word out of Abominadad is that Maddas Hinsein is dead. If he were not, why has his defense minister seized power?"

Idly the Master of Sinanju aimed a remote-control unit toward the nearby combination television and VCR unit. A tape began playing.

Smith watched intently as the last televised images out of Irait played again. He saw Remo pull back one arm to unleash the death blow that was meant to extinguish Don Cooder. Remo's hand, a spear of stiffened fingers, snapped out.

Too fast for even the camera to record it, a woman in a flowing black *abayuh* reached out to snatch Cooder from the blow's path. Remo's hand kept going, striking the grinning mustached figure in the green burnoose that stood directly behind.

"That man was not Maddas Hinsein," Chiun informed Smith as the tall burnoosed form was blown out of the frame with bone-breaking force.

"Why do you say that?" Smith asked as the camera caught a glimpse of the woman in the *abayuh* as she lifted her garment to expose her naked form and spidery limbs.

"Because," Chiun said, hitting the pause button, "*that* is Maddas Hinsein."

Smith leaned into the screen, blinking owlishly.

In one corner of the frozen image, a second *abayuh*-clad figure was vaulting over the reviewing-stand rail. Smith saw clearly the shiny black paratroop boots under the garment's wildly lifting hem.

"Boots," Smith said. "Very interesting, but hardly proof positive."

Wordlessly Chiun tapped the off switch and returned to his labors.

Noting the cool blue glow of the Sterno fire, Smith said, "I trust the wok was sufficient for your needs. Finding a brass brazier on short notice was not possible."

"We shall see if it accomplishes its purpose," was all the Master of Sinanju would say.

"The President has not yet made a military decision," Smith said when the silence had grown long. "The Hamidi officer in charge of the multinational coalition, Prince General Sulyeman Bazzaz, has refused to allow our forces to move. Politically, the President is stymied."

"Tell me of the other forces," Chiun suggested, still working on his scroll, which lay flat with its corners slightly curled under the weight of four stones.

"Well, currently the U.S.-led coalition includes the Hamidis, the Egyptians, the Syrians, the—"

"Speak to me not of Arab forces," Chiun snapped. "They are like the desert sands once the storm of war commences. They will sting the eyes and drag down the feet of your soldiers—those who do not turn against you."

"Well, there are the British, the French, the Greeks,

the Italians, the Poles, the Canadians, and other European elements."

Chiun looked up. "No Mongols?" he squeaked in surprise.

"No Mongolian units were available to us."

"I do not mean uniformed footmen," Chiun retorted, "but sturdy horse Mongols."

"We do have the Turks on our side," Smith offered.

"Turks are acceptable," Chiun sniffed, "if one plans a slaughter."

"The President is hoping to avoid any deaths."

"Then he is unworthy of being President. For the enemy enjoys carnage and will only be halted by his own destruction."

Chiun made a final dot on the scroll and left it to dry.

At that moment a furious crackling came from the covered wok.

"Ah," said Chiun, turning his attention to the fire. "It is done."

"I will leave you to your meal, then," Smith said, a trace of disappointment in his tone.

The Master of Sinanju lifted a frail hand whose long nails were like horn projections from which the flesh was retreating.

He said, "Hold, Emperor Smith."

Lifting the wok's brass lid, he laid it aside.

At the Master of Sinanju's beckon, Smith drew near. He leaned over the wok, from which steam and a faintly distasteful aroma rose.

"Isn't that—?" Smith began to say.

With his bare hands, Chiun lifted a tortoiseshell. Moisture beaded up from its humped dorsal surface. It was an odd rusty color, and speckled with brown leopardlike spots. Hairline cracks started from either edge. They radiated toward the dividing depression like thunderbolts in conflict. Here and there, they crossed.

"Show this to the general who commands your forces," Chiun directed.

Smith blinked.

"But what is it?" he blurted.

"It is a tortoiseshell," said the Master of Sinanju in a bland voice as he replaced the wok cover.

"I know that. I obtained it for you. But what is its significance?"

"The general will understand. Now, please leave me. I am weary from my labors."

"As you wish, Master Chiun," Harold Smith said in a puzzled voice. He went away, carrying the hot smelly object in ginger fingers.

The next morning a UPS express courier delivered the tortoiseshell in a nondescript Jiffy mailer to a side door of the White House.

The President of the United States himself signed for the package. He opened it, and even though he knew what to expect within, he still found himself turning the cracked and shriveled tortoiseshell over and over in his hands.

"I don't get it," muttered the President.

A moment later, the tortoiseshell in one hand and the cherry-red CURE line in the other, he was repeating himself to Harold Smith.

"I don't get it." His voice was as bewildered as a child lost in a mall.

"Nor do I," sighed Harold Smith. "But I would do as Master—"

"—The Oriental."

"—instructs. He has never failed us before."

"But this smacks of voodoo. How will it look to our coalition allies?"

"Like voodoo," Smith admitted. "On the other hand, what do you have to lose?"

"You have a point there," said the President, shoving

the tortoiseshell back into its Jiffy bag. "The ways things stand, we're on the brink of the biggest military conflagration since the Big One."

"Good luck, Mr. President."

The Jiffy bag was couriered over to the Pentagon by a military attaché and presented to the Joint Chiefs of Staff.

Down in the Tank—the Pentagon's war room—the Joint Chiefs lowered the lights before they extracted the withered shell for examination.

No one spoke for many minutes. Finally the chairman personally brought up the lights.

He held the shell up so that everyone could see, clearly and absolutely, that it was a tortoiseshell that seemed to have lain in the sun too long.

"Looks like the back off a turtle," the chief of staff of the Air Force ventured.

This seemingly safe opinion was contradicted all around. Some said it was a turtle shell. Others that it wasn't a shell at all but something else. No one one knew exactly what.

The chairman left the growing disagreement and got on the horn to the White House. He identifed himself, asked a silent question, and listened intently for several moments before hanging up.

"What did he say?" asked the commandant of the Marine Corps.

"He said, 'Never mind what it is, ship the damned thing.' Unquote."

A C-130 Hercules Transport left Andrews Air Force Base within the hour, a Pentagon courier seated on a web seat, an attaché case across his back and the tortoiseshell inside the case. The attaché believed he was carrying all-important Pentagon campaign plans for the defense of Hamidi Arabia and the liberation of occupied Kuran. He believed this because no less than the chairman of the Joint Chiefs of Staff had implied this. The chairman was not about to inform the man that he was ferrying the cracked shell of a tortoise—or possibly a turtle—all the way to a frontline base in the Hamidi desert.

Neither the attaché nor the chairman knew that that was exactly what lay within the attaché case.

# 6

Prince General Suleyman Bazzaz was, strictly speaking, neither a general nor a prince.

As the adopted son of Sheik Abdul Hamid Fareem, the title of prince was conferred upon him one night in a bedouin tent with only the hissing of sand-driven wind and the spitting of single-humped dromedaries as a musical accompaniment.

When this was done, Sheik Fareem clapped his withered hands together and asked his new son, "Your heart's desire. Name this thing and it will be done."

Since Sheik Fareem ruled over a stretch of sand under which the world's energy requirements slept, Prince Bazzaz thought carefully upon this.

"I have always wished to fly the great fighter jets," said the new prince, then but nineteen and fresh from a trip to Bahrain, where he had seen the forbidden-to-Moslems film called *Top Gun*—forbidden because it showed actual kissing. "My favorite is the F-14 Tomcat, a magnificent plane, for it boasts more fins than a 1957 Cadillac."

"You wish only to join the Royal Hamidi Air Force?" asked the sheik, a trace of disappointment creeping over his wind-seared old visage.

"No," said Prince Bazzaz, sensing that he was underestimating the offer before him. "I wish for my own aircraft carrier."

No sound passed between the two men in the candle-flicker light of the midnight tent. It was winter. The cruel northern wind, the *shamal*, threatened the sturdy tent.

Presently Sheik Fareem nodded mutely and stole from the tent. Outside, a retinue of servants and military guards awaited. At a gesture from their sheik, one proffered a cellular telephone. The sheik spoke nervously for some minutes into this and then returned to the striped tent.

"It will take five years to build one," Sheik Fareem explained in disappointment. "What would you do in the meantime?"

"I would be general of the Hamidi Royal Air Force."

"No," said the sheik, shaking his head. "I cannot allow any son of mine, even if his blood is not my own, to be a mere general."

Prince Bazzaz's bronzed young face fell.

"No," the sheik went on sagely, "you shall be prince general."

Prince General Bazzaz' face lit up. That he had no experience in military service, never mind generaling, was of no moment, the sheik patiently explained to him.

"For as long as the black gold oozes up from the sands of Araby, the Americans will protect us," he had prophesied.

And so they did.

When the legions of the brutal Iraiti regime rolled south along the Irait-Kuran Friendship Road, slaughtering and looting and raping as they shouted their solidarity with Arabs everywhere, Prince General Suleyman Bazzaz received the news at a difficult moment. It was while he was working on his tan.

The aide came to his private tanning booth in downtown Nemad, capital of Hamidi Arabia. It had cost twenty thousand dollars and gave almost as smooth a tan as the prince general would had gotten from sitting on a $12.95 chaise lounge under the scorching Hamidi sun. But even the lowliest *effendis* had the sun to bronze them. Only Bazzaz had a private tanning booth.

"The Iraitis are coming!" the aide shouted. "They have smashed into Kuran!"

"Our Kurani brothers will stop them," Prince General Bazzaz murmured nonchalantly. "They are almost as rich as we and they possess American weapons nearly the equal of our own."

"Which weapons are now in Iraiti hands," the aide added breathlessly. "And crack Iraiti Renaissance Guard units are heading this way."

Behind protective goggles of red lenses, the prince general's dark eyes blinked. "What of the valiant Kuranis?"

"Valiantly offering their services to protect our mutual border now that they have no country of their own," replied the aide.

Prince General Bazzaz threw off his protective visor and hurried into a white uniform which would have made an opera star blush with embarrassment and was whisked to the sheik's palace in his personal motorcade.

He arrived in exactly five minutes, three more than if he had walked. The palace was directly across the street from the command headquarters. But the winds were up and he did not wish to get dust on his ivory-white paratroop boots.

"O long-lived one," Bazzaz cried, bursting in on the *majlis*, where the sheik heard the complaints—which were many—of his people, "I am told the Iraitis have stabbed our Kurani brothers in the back."

"Let the word go forth," said the sheik, indignation making his voice quake. "This is an Arab affair. No outsiders are to meddle in matters between our brothers."

"Their tanks are coming this way. They covet our land. I have never before fought a war, O Father. What do

I do? Which uniform should I wear—the white or the gold?"

The sheik blinked. He drew his adopted son close and whispered in his ear, "Call the Americans. Only they can save us now."

"But what about our Arab honor?" Bazzaz had demanded. "What about my honor? I am commander in chief."

"Honor is but a word," hissed the sheik. "Our blood is as spillable as any Kurani's. Call the Americans, and be silent. We will talk of honor once our nation is again secure."

And so began the mightiest airlift in history.

By the time the Hamidi-Kuran border had been fortified with several U.S. divisions and Hamidi Arabia at least temporarily secure from invasion, the question of command was first raised.

"I will command," said Prince General Bazzaz smoothly, upon meeting the general in charge of the UN forces. Today he was wearing the gold uniform, having decided to alternate.

"It's my army," retorted General Winfield Scott Hornworks, supreme commander of Allied Forces Central Command.

"It is my nation," said the prince general, who did not immediately comprehend why the unbeliever did not obey instantly. Had his father not hired this infidel army to do the will of the Hamidi royal family?

"Fine," retorted General Winfield Scott Hornworks. "We'll be on our way home, seeing as how your nice little sandbox of a country is out of immediate danger. If the Iraitis act up again, you give us a yell, hear?"

Prince General Bazzaz' eyes fixed on the broad retreating back of the American general as he started out of the room, looking like a human chocolate-chip cookie in his desert utilities and bush hat. They grew wide like twin explosions of surprise as the general's words sank in.

"I have a brilliant idea!" he called, lifting his bejeweled swagger stick. It trembled.

The general half-turned. "If it's half as brilliant as that getup of yours," he said dryly, "it oughta be a doozy."

"Why do we not rotate?"

"Rotate what?"

"Our responsibilities," Bazzaz said, smiling weakly. "Twelve hours for you and twelve for me."

Since the general had not actually been authorized to withdraw from Hamidi Arabia and was hoping to bluff the prince general, he gave this proposition serious thought. "It's possible," he allowed at last.

"Excellent! I will take days. I am a day person. Not a night oil."

"That's 'owl' and you got yourself a deal," said the general, who figured even in the crazy event the Pentagon went for this arrangement, any first strike would be a night operation.

"I would shake on it," said the prince general, "but you look like a pork-eater. No offense."

"None taken. And I got enough of a lungful of your perfume at this distance."

"It is English Leather," said the prince general proudly.

"You musta got the industrial-strength version," returned Hornworks dryly.

To General Winfield Scott Hornworks' utter astonishment, the Pentagon had gone for the insane shared-command idea.

"It's politically expedient," the U.S. secretary of defense had told him.

"Let me speak to the JCS," snapped General Hornworks, who decided to appeal to someone with sense and a uniform.

The chairman of the Joint Chiefs of Staff was equally supportive of the shared-command concept.

"And what the hell do I do if this goes to conflict?" roared General Hornworks.

"That won't happen. Maddas Hinsein isn't that crazy, to take on the U.S. in open conflict."

Except that as the weeks rolled by, it looked more and more as if he was. He had taken hostage every Westerner in Irait. He began threatening Israel. He promised a global conflagration if the U.S. did not withdraw from the gulf region. And when the Iraiti ambassador to the U.S. had been found strangled by a yellow ribbon, he had attempted to have two of the most prominent Western hostages publicly executed.

It was the eleventh month of the crisis. Word came from the U.S. President to prepare to begin the run-up to liberate Kuran.

Unfortunately, the execute order came at 2:36 P.M. Hamidi Gulf Time, while Prince General Suleyman Bazzaz was technically in command of the Star in the Center of the Flower of the East Military Base, a sprawling command post north of Nehmad.

"Absolutely not," sniffed the prince general, who was redolent of Old Spice on this day. This was a concession to the Americans, who had been driven to fits of retching by prolonged exposure to excessive amounts of Engish Leather. They were wearing out their gas-attack equipment.

"What do you mean?" roared General Hornworks. "That was a direct order from our commander in chief!"

"*Your* commander in chief," Bazzaz said with cool unconcern. "To us, he is hired help."

General Hornworks had to be restrained from strangling the prince general on the spot. Recognizing two things despite his lack of military background—that his life was in mortal peril and that once his watch was over, the infidel general was certain to execute the insane order of the United States President—Prince General Suleyman Bazzaz did the only thing that to him made tactical sense.

He had the general clapped in irons.

Then he called his father, the sheik.

"You have done well, my son," said Sheik Fareem. "I can see the day when you will stand proud as sheik general."

"May your greatness increase, O Father," said the prince general. "What do we do now?"

"We will not risk a foolhardy war over the spoiled Kuranis. Instead, we must have patience and trust in Allah. Something will come up."

The hoped-for something came by U.S. military plane a day later.

A smartly dressed Pentagon attaché asked to speak with General Hornworks. It was not yet dawn, so this was no insult to Prince General Bazzaz, otherwise he would have found himself in chains as well.

"General Hornworks has been disposed of," he told the attaché.

"You mean he's indisposed?" asked the man, thinking he had encountered nothing more than the expected language barrier.

Bazzaz had to think about that one. "Yes, I mean that. You may deliver your message to me, the prince general in charge of UN Central Command."

"I am sorry, General Prince—"

"Prince General."

"Prince General," went on the attaché in a polite robotlike tone that implied the prince general had no more standing than Whistler's mother. "But my orders are to deliver this briefcase to General Hornworks in person. It is urgent, sir."

Prince General Suleyman Bazzaz noticed that the man carried the briefcase manacled to one wrist. He contemplated accusing the attaché of theft, which would give him a wonderful excuse to chop off the infidel's hand and not have to fuss with the doubtless complicated lock.

Further consideration brought him to the reluctant conclusion that even if he did that, there was still the matter of the briefcase lock. War was such a tiresome affair, he concluded.

"Come, then," Prince General Bazzaz said stiffly.

The attaché was escorted to the general's basement cell. He didn't blink an eye when he saw his superior behind iron bars.

"This is for you, sir," he said, snapping to rigid attention, the briefcase held out in stiff arms.

"You can hold that pose until the desert turns to glass," General Hornworks said acidly, "but as long as those bars are between me and that briefcase, there's not a dang thing I can do about it."

"I will agree to open the cell," Prince General Bazzaz said, "if my American counterpart will agree to abide by my every wish."

"Eat sand."

Bazzaz stiffened. He was not sure what would happen if he unlocked the cell, but the contents of the briefcase intrigued him.

"I would open this cell as a gesture of solidarity, and trust to your good instincts, even though you are a consumer of pork chops and bacon, if only you would agree not to harm me."

General Hornworks' eyes narrowed craftily. "Done," he said quickly. "I ain't one for holding a grudge."

"Excellent."

The prince general signaled the turnkey. The cell opened.

The American general stepped out. Silently, he took the briefcase and unlocked it with a key the attaché silently handed to him.

Out of the briefcase came the leopard-spotted tortoiseshell.

With a hangdog expression on his square-jawed features, General Winfield Scott Hornworks turned the cracked, desiccated shell over in his hands as if that would somehow activate it.

"This thing's just a goldurn turtle shell," he muttered.

"Let me see that," said Prince General Bazzaz.

"See it?" snapped Hornworks. "You can keep it. It's nothing."

The prince general accepted the shell in his smooth hands. And with both of his callused hands, Hornworks shoved him into the cell he had just vacated. He kicked the door closed.

"Now it's your turn," he snorted.

"You are not authorized to do this," Bazzaz protested, grabbing the bars. He let go when he realized he was getting rust on his immaculate sleeves. "It is day."

Hornworks looked around the dim cellblock. "Sure looks like night to me." He eyed the attaché. "Wouldn't you say, soldier?"

"Yes, sir, it's definitely dark," said the attaché. "Pitch."

"Let me out! This is an outrage!"

"What're you beefing about?" growled General Hornworks. "You got your durn turtle shell."

Bazzaz looked down. In the wavering light he examined the cracked shell. He turned it like a compass, as if recognizing it.

As the American general and his attaché walked away, he called after him.

"Wait! I understand now!"

"Glad to hear it." The general chuckled. "Next war, we might even get along."

"No. This shell, it contains the secret! I know what to do now." The prince general's voice skittered excitedly.

General Hornworks stopped dead in his tracks. He turned.

"If this is a trick," he warned, "I'm gonna reach my hands in through those bars and throttle you good."

"Truly, it is not a trick. Look!" The prince general held the tortoise shell in the light.

"Looks like a mud turtle after a deuce-and-a-half squashed it into Tennessee roadkill," Hornworks concluded.

"Examine the cracks. Please," pleaded the prince general.

Frowning, Hornworks returned to the bars. He leaned down to see better in the weak light.

"Explain it to me," he muttered.

The prince general used a shaking-with-excitement beringed finger to trace a line across the length of the shell.

"Behold!" he said proudly. "This is the border with our country and unfortunate Kuran. And this long brown shape must be the infamous Maddas Line."

"Naw, it's a squiggle of color put there by nature."

"Allah put it there, and Allah does not roll dice."

"Baloney."

"Is that pork?" Bazzaz asked, wrinkling his hooked nose.

"Search me. What are these cracks?"

"These are lines of attack. See, they are coming from the north. They obviously represent tank and soldier queues."

"Mechanized and infantry columns," said Hornworks thoughtfully. They did look pretty realistic at that.

"And these," Bazzaz said excitedly. "See those lines that drive up to strike the Iraiti lines? These are counterattacks."

Hornworks blinked. He leaned closer. They did kinda have that look. In fact, the strategy was pretty damn strack.

General Hornworks caught himself. "Wait a chicken-scratching minute," he exploded, straightening. "These are just cracks."

"If this is so, why did your Paragon—"

"Pentagon."

"—send this to you by messenger?"

That was a point General Winfield Scott Hornworks had no clear answer to.

"What're you suggesting?" he asked at last.

"If these lines mean that Irait will attack here, here, and here," Bazzaz said, indicating the border line, "we must arrange our peoples."

"Forces."

"To intercept their charges here, here, and there."

General Hornworks looked askance. "I'll buy that on one condition," he cautioned.

"Speak this thing," Bazzaz said sincerely.

"That nobody, but nobody, hears about our little *tête-à-tête.*"

"You mean strategy session."

"No, I mean *tête-à*-dang-*tête*," said General Hornworks, signaling the turnkey. "I could be cashiered for what I'm about to do."

As they walked from the dungeon, the all-important tortoiseshell passing back and forth between them, Prince General Suleyman Bazzaz made a mournful comment.

"It is unfortunate the Iraitis did not wait another three years before attacking."

"Yeah?" his American counterpart growled. "Why's that?"

"Because by then I would have had my own personal aircraft carrier and your services would not even have been necessary."

# 7

They were lost in Abominadad. It was easy to become lost in Abominadad. Every building boasted a huge portait of Maddas Hinsein, wearing a bewildering assortment of uniforms. And even though he seemed to have more changes of clothes than Imelda Marcos had shoes, it was still not as many uniforms as Abominadad had buildings.

"I think the American embassy is around this next corner," Don Cooder ventured.

"Yeah? What makes you say that?" asked Reverend Juniper Jackman.

"Last time I was here, the U.S. embassy was around the corner from a picture of President Hinsein dressed as a biblical warrior riding a chariot."

Reverend Jackman looked up. Sure enough, there was Maddas Hinsein, flogging a team of horses like an out-of-shape extra from *Ben Hur*.

Cooder led the way around the corner. The bags under his eyes seemed to melt in disappointment as they encountered a sun-bleached mosque.

"If that's our embassy," Reverend Jackman said sourly, "we're definitely in the wrong pew."

"I think we're lost," muttered Don Cooder.

"I think you're right."

They paused in the shadow of the mosque. The clatter

of Hind gunships came from somewhere over the rooftops. It did not quite drown out the deafening clash and clangor of those giant scimitars, still going at one another with a ferocity equal to an ancient Armageddon.

"Tell me," Cooder said, his eyes haunted. "Do those sound like our helicopters or theirs?"

"You tell me, you're the ace newshound."

"I just read copy."

They heard a racket of rockets and machine guns.

Then, one by one, the fireballs lifted over the rooftops.

"We're being nuked!" Don Cooder howled.

"The Bible was right!" Reverend Jackman screamed, sounding as surprised as a man could be. "The world's gonna end in the Middle East!"

Which was precisely the thought racing through the dazed mind of Maddas Hinsein when he witnessed the identical sight. He had stumbled through the souks and byways of downtown Abominadad in his frayed *abayuh* until he had come to a movie theater which played, by presidential decree, a perpetual double bill consisting of *The Godfather*, parts one and two. They were Maddas Hinsein's favorite films.

Maddas had ducked into the theater's welcome darkness. It was deserted, so he took a seat in the center of the first row.

As it happened, he came in on the scene where Don Corleone first mumbled the immortal line, "I'm gonna make you an offer you can't refuse."

Under his concealing veil, the big brown eyes of the Scimitar of the Arabs misted over. He had sent his foreign minister to a summit with the now-deposed Emir of Kuran with instructions to deliver that very line at exactly high noon.

When the emir had refused Irait's generous offer to surrender the vital Homar oilfield and a pair of unimportant islands to Irait, despite his own nation's heavy indebtedness to Kuran, the foreign minister had broken off talks, as instructed.

Obviously the emir had not been a movie buff. He had missed the very clear diplomatic signal.

The first Iraiti tank divisions rolled through Kuran within twenty minutes of that pretext of a meeting. They advanced, as one newspaper had put it, "as if laying down blacktop, not waging war."

Don Corleone knew how to motivate men, thought Maddas Hinsein as the flickering screen images filled him with nostalgia.

Unfortunately, Maddas Hinsein did not know how to run a movie projector. The reel ran out, leaving the engrossed Scimitar of the Arabs blinking at a blindingly white screen. He cursed the lack of a projectionist. The man had deserted his post. When he was restored to power, Maddas promised himself, he would have the slacker hanged for dereliction of duty.

It was as he stumbled out into the deserted streets that Maddas Hinsein saw the first fireball. It was like a fist of flame snaking skyward.

It looked exactly like a mushroom cloud.

"Impossible!" howled Maddas Hinsein. "It cannot be!"

There were two reasons for his hasty conclusion. First, he knew that these could not be U.S. nukes. The Americans had not the stomach to nuke Abominadad, he was certain. Of course, he had been equally certain that the U.S. would not bat an eyelash at his lightning annexation of Kuran. And before that, that his neighbor Irug could not resist his invading armies more than a month. A decade-long war that bankrupted both regimes had resulted.

Then another fireball blossomed before his veiled eyes like an angry flower.

"How can this be?" Maddas sputtered.

The second reason the sight of mushroom clouds stupefied the Scimitar of the Arabs was that he was certain they could not mark an Israeli attack. Not that the Jews would hesitate to strike. But that by now their entire leadership should be breathing Sarin, Tabun, and other fatal nerve gases.

For the deadfall commands President Maddas Hinsein had left with his loyal defense minister, Razzik Azziz, were explicit instructions to unleash war gases on Tel Aviv and other key Israeli installations via the dreaded al-Hinsyn missile.

"Traitor!" snarled Maddas Hinsein. "The coward has betrayed his heritage to save his worthless skin."

Gathering up the ebony folds of his *abayuh*, Maddas Hinsein stormed down the street.

Another mushroom cloud lifted into the air. The distant thunder of concussion shock blew glass out of windows, showering him with wicked shards. Miraculously, none struck him, which the Scimitar of the Arabs took as a sign from Allah.

His course took him past the sprawl of Maddas International Airport. What he beheld there stunned him to the core.

He saw Americans and Europeans, their faces alight with relief, stumbling from buses and official vehicles. They carried luggage. His own national police were escorting them to waiting planes lined up at terminals and on the runways as if anxious to carry the hostages to the outer world.

"More treachery," said Maddas Hinsein, reaching through a slit in his black garment to grasp the ivory grips of his personal sidearm.

He considered executing the traitors where they stood, but realized he had only six shots in his pistol, while they had AK-47 assault rifles.

Reversing direction, Maddas Hinsein retreated like a furtive black specter.

The fireballs had expended themselves, he saw. Except

for the regular roar of jet aircraft taking off, the city had grown quiet. It was like the lull before the storm.

As he rushed toward the U.S. embassy, the only source of hostages available to him, he vowed that Maddas Hinsein would be the storm of all storms.

# 8

The President of the United States received with profound relief the news of the exodus of what were diplomatically called "guests under duress" by the Iraitis and "hostages" by everyone else.

"This means we're out of the woods, doesn't it?" he suggested to his defense secretary.

"Yes," the man said firmly.

"No," inserted the chairman of the Joint Chiefs of Staff, just as firmly. His dark handsome face was stiff with resolve. As the first black to hold the position, he was not about to become a yes-man to the defense secretary, whom everyone knew harbored presidential aspirations. So did he, but he was too sophisticated a strategist to tip his hand in advance.

The President's brow furrowed. "No?"

"Look at these satellite recon photos," said the chairman, laying down a folder stamped "TOP SECRET" on the polished table.

They were down in the White House Situation Room. The red threat-condition lights were ablaze.

The President extracted the photos. He looked at the one on top. So did the defense secretary.

What they saw was an overhead shot of Abominadad. They knew it was Abominadad because of the unmistakable latticework of a roller coaster that had been inexpertly thrown up on the western outskirts of the city, near the fixed antimissile missile batteries. The roller coaster had been part of the loot of Kuran. Taking it down and transporting it overland had proved easier than putting it up correctly. Most of the tracks stopped in midair, as if bitten off.

Closer to the center of the city was a large area of debris, much like a crater. Smoke smudges billowed up from this area.

"What is it?" demanded the President, shifting to the next photo. It showed a slightly larger crater. As did the one below it.

"Arab Renaissance Square," reported the chairman. "You can see the mangled scimitar in the upper-right-hand corner."

"Looks like a pretzel," the defense secretary commented.

"What caused this?" asked the President.

"Unknown, sir. But whatever it is, it's getting wider. The CIA believes this is why the Iraitis are so hot to capitulate."

"This is why they've asked us to cease hostilities?" the President asked, dumbfounded.

"I believe so."

"But we haven't started hostilities. This isn't our doing."

"Must be the Israelis," said the defense secretary. "Their fingers have been on the trigger ever since this fracas started."

"If we ask nicely, do you think they'll stop?" the President wondered aloud.

The defense secretary called the secretary of state, who in turn called the Israeli ambassador to the U.S. Word was flashed to Tel Aviv and flashed instantly back.

"The Israelis say they are on stand-down," reported the defense secretary only nine minutes after the President had asked what had been a rhetorical question.

"The Iraitis blame us, huh?" the President said, laying aside the photos. "Is that good or bad?"

"If they consider it a provocation, they'll probably go to war over it. After all, Maddas is sandfill and Abombinadad is releasing everybody."

"Exactly why we should launch a preemptive strike," the chairman said firmly.

"Last time I did that," the President said ruefully, "the damn Hamidis blocked us."

The chairman cleared his throat. "I understand that situation has been rectified. General Hornworks is once again in control of the situation on the ground. He informs me that based on new intelligence findings, he has repositioned forward units to counter any Iraiti advance."

"What findings?" the President asked, raising one eyebrow.

The chairman of the Joint Chiefs of Staff placed his hands behind his back and regarded the scarlet ceiling. He declined to give a yes-or-no answer. It was the military way when confronted with the imponderable. Also, he figured it was even money he would run against the President next election. No sense providing a future political enemy with ammunition in the form of a directly attributable quote.

The President drew his defense secretary aside. "What do you think?"

"Diplomatically, so far we're winning. We're getting our hostages back. Maddas is wormfood. I say we press the advantage. Demand they withdraw unconditionally from Kuran."

Frowning, the President tapped the sheaf of recon photos. "What about this crater thing?"

The secretary of defense shrugged his shoulders. "That's out of my bailiwick," he told his commander in chief.

* * *

The President excused himself and, in the privacy of the Lincoln Bedroom, put the same question to Harold Smith.

"I can only assume that, er—"

"The Caucasian," interrupted the President.

"—is active in Abominadad," finished Smith. "Only he is capable of such unchecked carnage."

"What could he be up to?"

"It's impossible to say."

"Well, whatever he's doing," the President mused, "he's winning hands down. You should see those photos. Abominadad looks like an earthquake struck. Smith, can you deactivate him somehow?"

"Only the . . . Oriental might be able to accomplish that mission."

"Smith, get on it. Do whatever you have to. We have a chance to avert war here. But only if we move fast."

"I'll do what I can."

Harold Smith found the Master of Sinanju sitting up in bed watching a videotape.

As Smith entered, Chiun clicked the image off.

"You have been replaying the tapes?" Smith asked.

"I have been bored," Chiun said aridly. "The nurses do not comfort me as they should."

Smith cleared his throat. "I have heard from the President. He is gravely concerned. Some agency has created a crater in the middle of Abominadad."

Chiun's tight expression went slack. "The dance has begun."

"Master?"

"The Tandava. It is the dance that will destroy the world. Nothing can stop it. Kali has lured Shiva into the Tandava, despite his wishes to the contrary."

"I understand," said Smith in a tone that plainly said that he was not comfortable with that understanding. "I was about to ask you to stop Remo."

"He is no longer Remo and he cannot be stopped," Chiun said, brittle-voiced.

"The Iraitis are threatening war unless Remo ceases."

"The jest is on them. War or no war, they are doomed. And they will be only the first. Shiva and Kali will trample and snuff out all life on this forlorn globe."

"I am sorry to hear that," said Smith, for lack of anything better to say. A thought occurred to him. "I suppose you will wish to return to Sinanju."

"Why?"

"Why, to be with your people when the end comes. Unless you think Shiva will spare Korea?"

Chiun's hazel eyes narrowed. "No," he said, his voice growing steely. "Shiva will not spare Sinanju."

"Shall I arrange for a submarine passage home?" asked Smith.

"No," the old Korean said after a pause. "I wish a telephone. For I must contact certain allies."

"I can arrange that," Smith said crisply. "Anything else?"

"Yes. Send word to Sheik Abdul Hamid Fareem, of Hamidi Arabia."

Smith's lemony face puckered. "What word?"

"Tell him two things. One, the Master of Sinanju yet lives. And two, he is coming to parley."

"Does this mean you will need transportation to the Middle East?"

"That is the last thing I would have you do, Emperor Smith," said Chiun, closing his tired old eyes.

# 9

The call flashed eastward. It traveled along fiberoptic telephone cable from Folcroft Sanitarium, was microwaved to an orbiting satellite and bounced back to an earth station in the Far East, where the message was received, transcribed on a lambskin parchment in an ancient tongue, and carried by hand to the eyes for which it was intended.

The message was terse:

"Follow the Seven Giants to the Ishtar Gate. Bring the caliph's sack."

Wise eyes lifted skyward, where the stars continued in their ancient procession.

A voice was raised.

"I hear, and obey, friend of the old days," it said.

And then the thunder began to roll.

# 10

As they slunk through the streets of Abominadad, Don Cooder and Reverend Juniper Jackman noticed a strange thing.

Cars were streaming by. A constant parade of them. Buses too. Each was filled with Americans and other non-Arab nationals. All under heavily armed guard.

"What do you think's going on?" Reverend Jackman wondered in a low, uneasy voice.

"I think it's a mass execution," Cooder said. "They must be taking them to a central location. Probably in retaliation for the A-bombs that are dropping all over."

Reverend Jackman cupped a hand behind one ear. "I don't hear no more bombs, A, B, or C. And if I'm gonna be executed, it ain't gonna be with plain folks. I want center stage."

"And I want the U.S. embassy. We're public figures. They'll give us sanctuary."

"You mean they'll give *me* sanctuary," snapped Reverend Jackman. "But I'll try to put in a good word for you."

Arguing, they pushed on.

When they reached the U.S. embassy, they were shocked to their core to discover the main gate was chained closed.

"What's this?" Reverend Jackman bleated. His eyeballs protruded like shelled eggs being squeezed from fists.

Don Cooder's eyes, on the other hand, narrowed over his waxy bags as if not wishing to face reality.

Both men had to read the sign three times before its full import was brought home to them.

The sign read:

> ATTENTION, ALL CONCERNED:
>
> THE IRAITI GOVERNMENT HAS DECREED THAT ALL U.S. CITIZENS AND OTHER THIRD-STATE NATIONALS ARE FREE TO EVACUTE IRAIT. IF YOU FALL UNDER EITHER CATEGORY AND DESIRE EVACUATION, PROCEED IMMEDIATELY TO MADDAS INTERNATIONAL AIRPORT. THIS EMBASSY HAS BEEN CLOSED FOR THE DURATION OF HOSTILITIES.
>
> —THE U.S. AMBASSADOR

"Does this mean we're stranded?" asked Don Cooder in a tight dry voice.

Swallowing an indigestible lump in his throat, Reverend Juniper Jackman looked toward the west, where the airport lay.

An Air Irait 747 lifted off, trailing a sooty plume of exhaust. In a matter of seconds, another launched itself after the first. A third followed.

"Not yet," said Reverend Jackman. "But from the way they're hightailing it outta here, I'd say procrastinating ain't a good idea."

They stepped out into the street in search of a cab. Don Cooder whistled through a mouthful of fingers. Reverend Cooder, recalling the sixties, looked for a clean patch of asphalt where he could stage a one-man civil-disobedience sit-in.

Maddas Hinsein galumphed along like a big ungainly scarecrow draped in a black cape. His all-concealing veil lifted and fell with each puffing exhalation. He was running out of breath. Even though he had appointed himself field marshal of the Iraiti Armed Forces, he had never seen military service. Consequently he was a tad out of shape.

It happened that a green cab careened around a corner just as Maddas Hinsein had reached the limit of his endurance. Three short blocks.

He stepped out into the path of the cab, crying, "Halt!" in a high-pitched voice.

The cab screeched to a halt, the driver leaning out of the driver's window to hurl abuse at him.

"One side, *kebir gamoose!*" he yelled.

Maddas Hinsein strode up to the driver. Still keeping his voice high, he asked, "What did you call me, *effendi?*"

"I called you a big water buffalo," the other snarled. "Now, get out of my way. I have Americans to fetch. The new president has decreed that they be released before the bombs begin to fall."

"New president?" Maddas asked, for the first time noticing that the driver lacked the politically correct mustache all Iraiti men by law had to cultivate.

"Yes," the man said impatiently. "*Al-Ze'em.* Razzik Azziz."

"That is very interesting," said Maddas Hinsein, surreptitiously reaching into his *abayuh.* "But that name you called me—is is not the nickname certain disloyal elements have bestowed upon the last president?"

"He is dead, and Allah curse his bones," spat the driver. "Now, be off, woman. There is money to be made."

"And you have earned your last dinar, traitorous one," intoned Maddas Hinsein in his normal gruff tone. And he shot the cabdriver through the temple with such exquisite precision that both of the man's eyes were whisked from their sockets like magic.

Opening the door, the Scimitar of the Arabs reached

in to yank the corpse from his seat. He took the man's place. Such had been his skill that little blood and no brains decorated the front seat. Killing was one thing to Maddas Hinsein. Wallowing in the result, another.

Placing one heavy foot on the gas, he wrenched the wheel around. He was bound for the U.S. embassy, where no doubt the traitorous son of a pig had been headed. And woe to any American who fell into his hands.

It was not that there was any lack of taxicabs in the heart of Abominadad. There were plenty, Don Cooder and Reverend Jackman found. And they were all going the right way—to the airport.

The trouble, they discovered upon being ignored by the seventh speeding cab, was that they were all crammed to the windows with Western evacuees.

"Why do they got rides when we don't?" Reverend Jackman demanded from the safety of the curb. His sit-in had not survived his first brush with a cab's hurtling grille.

"Because you're still stuck in the sixties," Don Cooder said, determination creeping into his voice. "Watch how a nineties man does it."

He stepped out into the middle of the street. A cab came along. He lifted his arms and waved them frantically.

The cab slowed to a stop. The driver leaned on the horn.

Ignoring the sound, Don Cooder confidently strode over to the rear window. He knocked. It rolled down.

"Hi, I'm Don Cooder, legendary BCN anchorman," he said brightly.

"I don't have time to be interviewed," said the man in back. His Phillies baseball cap identified him as an American. "We're on the way to airport. They've set us free."

"Got room in back for two?" Cooder asked through a fixed smile.

"No. My wife is with me." A redhead with a drawn face gave him a brave little wave, adding, "I watch you all the time, Mr. Brokaw."

Pitching his voice lower, Cooder added, "How about just one?"

"Sorry. Driver, let's go. *Wallah!*"

Don Cooder had been holding on to the cab's chrome trim when the passenger gave the order. The trim was torn from his hands, taking part of a fingernail with it.

"Yeoow!" he screamed, anguish gullying his craggy features.

Reverend Jackman came running up, horror writ large on his own pop-eyed face.

"Are you shot? Did he shoot you?"

"A fingernail! I lost a fingernail! How will this look before America?"

Reverend Jackman put his hands on his hips and a frown on his face.

"You know what? You are wound tighter that the mainspring of my granddaddy's old turnip watch. Never mind your damn manicure. We gotta fetch us a ride."

"All America looks up to me for personal grooming guidance," said Don Cooder, sucking on the injured digit, which happened to be his thumb. He looked very comfortable sucking his thumb.

The next cab to come along actually slowed down when it saw them.

Reverend Jackman started for it. He saw the back seat was empty. His face exploded in pleasure.

"Hey, thumbsucker!" he called. "I got us a lift!"

Don Cooder looked up from the curb where he sat performing surgery on his ripped thumbnail with a small penknife.

"What say?"

"It's empty. Get your thumb out of your hole and your ass over here."

Cooder shot to his feet. In a flash, he was beside Jackman.

"We go to airport, savvy?" Jackman was saying to the driver.

Don Cooder shoved him aside, saying, "You don't say 'savvy,' you idiot. This is Irait. You say '*wallah*'!" He turned to the driver. "You, take us to the airport. *Wallah!*"

The driver regarded them through a dense mesh veil. For the first time they noticed that the figure behind the wheel was shrouded in the native costume of a Moslem woman.

"I thought women weren't allowed to drive in this country," Reverend Jackman muttered.

"That's down in Hamidi Arabia," Cooder retorted. He addressed the silent driver. "You! Maddas Airport. Got that? Maddas. Mad Ass. Savvy?"

"*La!* Maddas," said the driver. The shrouded head nodded eagerly.

"Great!" said Don Cooder. "She understands. Let's go."

They piled in back.

The cab got under way, tires squealing.

"This is great," chortled Reverend Jackman. "You done good. When I'm president, I might just have a place for you in my administration."

"President? You're dreaming. You're passé."

"You just lost a chance to be my press secretary," Reverend Jackman sniffed. "I'm a shoo-in next time. All I need is the black vote. That's almost forty percent if I can get them into the voting habit. Brother minorities, like the spics, wops, et cetera, should fetch me fifteen percent. Then I got the NOW vote. That's thirty-five percent. Those who watch my talk show. I got a two share. That's what? Two million? We'll call it four. I figure that's three percent of America. Then the liberals. Twenty percent for sure. And those who admit being liberals. A quarter of a percent."

"That's almost one hundred and fifteen percent!"

Reverend Jackman smiled confidently. "In like Flynn."

His smile went south when he noticed that the aircraft lifting off could not be seen through the windshield past the driver's head.

"Must be a lull," he remarked.

"Sure hope they didn't run plumb out of gas," added Cooder. "Gas has been drying up all over this town faster than cow piss on a flat rock."

Over the engine mutter they heard the continual roar of takeoffs.

Don Cooder looked out his window and Reverend Jackman his.

They saw no aircraft, although the intermittent roar continued.

Their eyes met, grew wide, and all at once they snapped their heads around to look out the rear window.

There, framed in the bouncing glass, was a climbing string of aircraft. They were all shapes and sizes. Large air buses. Small private ships. Even a couple of helicopters. It looked like the fall of Saigon.

Their heads whipped back around and they began accosting the silent driver.

"Hey, you! Islam. You're going the wrong way."

"Driver, turn around. You turn around right now. That's a direct order. I'm an American anchorman."

Don Cooder reached out to grab the driver's shoulder. He snagged instead the hood of the black garment. It came away in his grasping fingers.

"Now you done it," Reverend Jackman whispered. "I think what you just done is against the law in this place. In fact, it's practically rape or something."

"I don't care. I'm going to the airport. *Wallah! Wallah*! Turn around."

The driver did turn around finally. But not the way they expected. After braking the car abruptly, throwing Reverend Jackman and Don Cooder slamming facesfirst into the front-seat cushions, the driver himself turned around in his seat.

A vaguely familiar visage showed a broad smile and the manhole-size muzzle of a shiny pistol.

"*Bass!*" he said. They took that to mean "Settle down." They weren't far off.

After they had stopped bouncing back and forth in their seats, Reverend Jackman's eyes seized upon the face of the driver.

"You know," he hissed, "this guy ain't a he. He's a she."

Don Cooder swallowed. "Does she—I mean he—kinda look like Maddas Hinsein to you?"

"Kinda. But everybody in this neighborhood looks like Maddas."

Don Cooder licked his lips. "Maybe. But this guy really, really looks like ol' Mad Ass."

"Can't be. He's dead."

The cab started off again.

"If that ain't Mad Ass," Reverend Jackman wondered, "why ain't he taking us to the airport?"

"Don't say that. Don't even think it."

"I can't help it. My eyes are telling me one thing and my brain another."

The two men fell silent for several moments. Then Reverend Jackman offered another disheartening observation.

"Don't look now," he muttered, "but that's the Palace of Sorrows up ahead."

"You know any prayers?" asked Don Cooder.

"No. I do sermons, not prayers. There's no money in praying. Look at Mother Theresa. Can't hardly feed herself on what she earns praying. I ask you, what kinda life is that?"

# 11

Sheik Abdul Hamid Fareem was worried.

When he had wanted the U.S. to strike Irait first, they had hesitated, preferring to defeat Maddas Hinsein and his criminal hordes with sanctions. As if such dealings would not increase the Shame of the Arabs' appetite.

When Maddas had apparently been assassinated before a global television audience, Sheik Fareem had breathed a sigh of relief. He understood how it was in Irait. Maddas Hinsein ruled absolutely. His death would break the Iraiti will. Sheik Fareem saw the fine hand of Sinanju in these occurrences. Had he himself not greeted the white Master of Sinanju who was called Remo, and assisted him in entering occupied Kuran?

And there he was, attired as if a genie out of the *Arabian Nights*, extinguishing the Tyrant of Irait before all the world. It was good. The crisis had passed. The Americans had, for once, done the correct thing. They had sent the greatest assassin in all the world to work their will.

Yet in the aftermath, the U.S. President had immediately ordered his forward troops to mobilize for a bloody liberation drive into occupied Kuran, against all reason. Did he not understand that this was no longer necessary?

It was fortunate that his adopted son, the prince general, had had the foresight to revoke this command. It had bought them time.

Allah, as always, had provided. First with the immediate release of the hostages, and then with the mysterious secret offensive plans of the Iraiti invader.

The winds of war were being blown away like the sands of the desert. Soon there would be peace.

Then further word had come from Washington, in the form of a private communication from the President himself. It had been hand-delivered by the U.S. ambassador. The text was brief.

"The one known to you as Chiun requests an audience. He will arrive shortly."

Upon reading these words, Sheik Fareem looked up, his wizened old face screwing into a dry pucker of confusion.

"What madness is this?" he muttered, stroking his beard. "Master Chiun is dead."

He ruminated upon this, drinking watered yogurt and fingering ivory worry beads, and decided the only answer was an unfortunate one. He was in league with the deranged. First they wanted war. Then they did not. Now they claimed to be sending him a dead man.

The sheik made a phone call. He was told that the personal aircraft carrier commissioned for his adopted son was still three years away from completion.

"I will pay triple if you deliver by Wednesday," the sheik implored.

"Impossible," said the shipyard supervisor. "You don't crank out an aircraft carrier like a stock car."

"Quadruple."

"Your highness, if I could I would."

"All right," the sheik said testily. "Quintuple! But no higher, you bandit!"

"I'd love to take your money," the man said sincerely, "but it's impossible. We just can't deliver an aircraft carrier on such short notice."

"Somewhere," growled Sheik Abdul Hamid Fareem just before he hung up the phone, "there is someone who can." He knew the white was lying. But he would not pay two billion dollars for a mere aircraft carrier. The prince general would have to wait. And the House of Hamid would have to find a way to solve this matter through the Americans.

When, hours later, the Master of Sinanju was announced, Sheik Fareem awoke with a start.

"Show him in," said the sheik, gathering his red-and-brown-striped *thobe* about his body, for he trembled in anticipation.

And upon beholding the sight of a short, wrinkled visage he had thought never again to see again in life, the sheik wept tears of joy and cried, "Master of Sinanju! Boundless is my joy on this day. For only you can assist me. I am beset my madmen."

*"Salaam Aleikim,"* intoned the Master of Sinanju gravely. "I have come to deal with the madman known as Maddas Hinsein. For he has cost me my only son."

The sheik started.

He said, "Maddas is dead. Which I believed you to be, as well. As for your son, I know only that he was the perpetrator of that glorious deed."

Chiun shook his age-racked head.

"No. The evil one lives. As for my son, he is beyond salvation. For he has fulfilled his ultimate destiny at last. As for me, I have come back from the very Void to deal with these things."

Sheik Fareem compressed his lips into a thin line. His ancestors had come to power with Dar al-Sinanju—the House of Sinanju—by their side. They had waxed powerful under their guidance. Their enemies had fallen like the sugar dates from the palms when the Masters of Sinanju of old had willed it.

Before him stood a man who looked a thousand years older than when last they met less than a decade ago.

The man he had believed dead. Now he resembled a mummy come back to life. There was no spark in his eyes. No vibrancy in his low, squeaky voice.

It was as if all the juices of life had been squeezed from the old Korean, leaving only a steely purpose and no hope, no joy at all.

"What is your desire, friend of my forefathers?" Sheik Fareem asked at last.

"It may be a war is to be fought. You will need a general."

"I have a general, my adopted son. He is—"

"For what is coming," Chiun said, "you will need a general like none to be found in your kingdom. Warriors such as have not trodden these deserts in many generations."

"Name these great ones."

"I," said the Master of Sinanju steadily, "am the general of Hamidi Arabia's salvation. As for the warriors, their name is so dreadful even I dare not speak it to you."

The sheik touched his chest, chin, and forehead in the traditional salute.

"It shall be as you wish, ally of my forefathers."

# 12

Wang Weilin was the first one to hear the sound.

It began as a distant hum. It was in his ears for many minutes before the eternal thunder—in the years to come, he would refer to the phenomenon in exactly those words—intruded upon his brain.

He was a peasant, was Wang Weilin. He squatted by the side of the road where his Flying Pigeon bicycle had struck the sharp rock that flattened his front tire.

He had no spare and the road was ill-traveled, so Wang had squatted by the roadside to smoke patiently as he awaited a passerby who might assist him.

When the eternal thunder first penetrated his morose thoughts, Wang stood up, casting his narrow darting eyes in all directions.

He saw nothing at first. Then, north, somewhere beyond the Tianshan Mountains, there was dust. Just dust.

"*Karaburan,*" he murmured. But it was not the Black Hurricane of the desert, he realized a moment later.

The thunder swelled. It did not rumble or gobble, or change tone or pitch in any way. It was steady. It drummed. Gods drumming on great iron rice bowls might have produced this thunder.

It disturbed Wang Weilin for some reason. Its very inexplicability was disheartening.

The dust continued to lift. Whatever phenomenon was

producing it, it was many miles away. Yet the wind carried some of the dust to his nostrils, and with it an unpleasant odor. It was not an odor Wang would naturally associate with the gods. It was animallike, distasteful. Tigers on the prowl might smell so. Or perhaps, he thought—his superstitious nature asserting itself—so might dragons.

Whatever it was—gods, demons, or dragons—it was following the old Silk Road that Marco Polo had once plied. And it was grinding westward.

And as it passed due north of Wang Weilin, another sound lifted over the thunder.

It was eerie, melodic. Unlike the thunder, this was not a constant sound. It undulated. And could only have been produced by a living throat.

But what throat? Wang Weilin thought, his heart skipping a beat. For the sound was huge, gargantuan, and in spite of its haunting beauty, threatening.

Thinking again of dragons, Wang Weilin threw away his Blue Swallow cigarette and grabbed up his Flying Pigeon bicycle by the handles.

He would push the balky thing all the way back to the village of Anxi, he vowed.

Even though Anxi was due east, in the opposite direction from which he had been traveling.

For if the singing dragon was bound west, Wang Weilin was going east. He did not wish to feed that melodious full-throated song with his mortal bones.

# 13

General Winfield Scott Hornworks was adamant.

"I do not take orders from sheiks, prince generals or . . ." He groped for a polite word. None came. "Whatever the heck you are."

"I am the Master of Sinanju," said the tiny little Asian guy who looked like death warmed over. He wore a kimono of raw silk. It was the color of a shroud. He stood with his sleeves joined together, his hands tucked inside.

"I especially do not take orders from Masters of Sinanju, whatever that may be," Hornworks added.

The old Asian cocked his head to one side. 'You are a soldier?"

"Ninth generation. A Hornworks fought with General Washington at Valley Forge."

"A Master of Sinanju stood at the throne of Pharaoh Tutankamen, with Cyrus the Great, Lord Genghis Khan, and others of equal stature."

General Winfield Scott Hornworks' blocky jaw dropped. He shut it. The sand fleas loved open mouths.

"You got me outflanked and outranked ancestry-wise," he gulped. He doffed his campaign hat in sincere salute.

They were standing outside Central Command Headquarters in the Star in the Center of the Flower of the

East Military Base. Patriot missile batteries ringed the perimeter, to protect against incoming Iraiti rocketry.

The sheik had had a tent erected beside a Patriot radar array for this meeting. They were outside the tent now. Prince General Bazzaz looked lost and unhappy standing beside his adoptive father.

"O long-lived one," he began, "I agree with the infidel general. I do not see the reason why—"

"Silence," said the sheik, chopping off the sentence with a swipe of his hand. "I command obedience." He turned to the American general. "As for you, your President, my ally, has commanded that you defer to the Master of Sinanju."

General Hornworks squared his star-bedizened epaulets. "I gotta hear that from the President himself."

The sheik snapped his fingers. A cellular telephone was slapped into his upraised hand. He worked it briefly, spoke, and then handed it to General Hornworks.

The general no sooner said, "Howdy," than he snapped to attention. "Yes, sir," he barked. "No, sir," he added. "Of course, sir," he concluded. "You got it. In spades."

Hitting the disconnect button, he returned the phone to the sheik. His broad features were sheepish. He swallowed uncomfortably.

"Are we in agreement?" asked the sheik in an age-cracked voice.

"Absolutely," said General Winfield Scott Hornworks, who knew exactly on which side his bread was buttered. Especially after his commander in chief had reminded him in a testy voice.

"Summon your lackeys," said the one called Chiun.

Hornworks assumed a blank expression. "My which?"

"Your lackeys," repeated the sheik, who wondered if the infidel general was hard of hearing.

Hornworks gulped. "Sir?"

"Your officers," the prince general put in, recognizing

that the infidel general was somehow under the impression he was not a mere paid mercenary.

"Oh. Officers. Why didn't you say so?"

No one offered an answer. They could see the American was suffering delusions of equality—a very common Western mental affliction for which there was no known cure.

They convened around the war room deep in the basement of the UN Central Command Building. The sheik sat silently, toying with his worry beads.

As they settled on the rug, forming a semicircle around the Master of Sinanju, the prince general went among them, handing out crisp white sheets of paper to each.

"What's this?" General Hornworks growled, turning the sheet this way and that.

"We will come to that later," said the Master of Sinanju. 'First, I must know several things. Your forces. They have been placed according to the tortoise's prediction?"

General Hornworks' eyes went wide. "Prediction! That was you?"

The Master of Sinanju nodded.

"We did it. Yeah. It was crazy, but the deployment was brilliant. What I don't quite get is why you scratched it on the back of a dead turtle."

"I did not," snapped Chiun. "Your forces will remain in place. There will be no advance unless attacked, no retreat under any circumstances."

"Nobody's going anywhere," General Hornworks vowed.

Chiun nodded. "Tell me of the dangers you face."

"Well," said General Hornworks, counting off on his fingers, "there's about, oh, fifty thousand dug-in Iraitis camped out in Kuran. Most of them's cannon fodder, you understand. They got their best units—"

"Legions. You will use correct military terms."

"We say 'units.' "

"You will say 'legions' as long as I am general," said Chiun stiffly.

Interest flickered in General Hornworks' blocky face. "Who died and made you general? I don't see any stars on your dang shoulders."

The old Korean narrowed his eyes. "You wish stars?"

"I'd like to see a few, yeah."

The Master of Sinanju obliged with a quick strike at the general's exposed forehead that sent Hornworks rocking back on his broad posterior.

Sure enough, he saw stars. He thought he heard birds too. Just like in a cartoon. They sounded like canaries.

"Are those stars sufficient to satisfy you?" asked the Master of Sinanju.

"Plenty," Hornworks croaked, holding his head. In fact, he was obviously outranked three to one. He hadn't even seen the old guy move.

"Continue your accounting of forces," Chiun commanded.

"Irait's got about five tank divisions in Kuran. And I'd say half that in Irait itself. But that ain't the biggest problem we got."

"What is?"

"Them damn Scud missiles of his. He's got maybe three hundred of them. Each one of them with enough range to hit us, Israel, or any other damn place in this sandbox of a region. No offense, Prince General."

"The opinions of pork-eaters cannot offend me," Prince General Bazzaz said with studied equanimity.

"Spoken like a true ally of America," Hornworks remarked.

"These Crud missiles," continued Chiun. "How best to render them harmless?"

Hornworks considered. "We could take 'em out by air strikes. But they're mobile. No way we can hit them all in one sortie raid. Some of them are bound to launch. And that would be one hellacious rain."

The Master of Sinanju stroked his wispy beard in thought, saying, "No, this must be done quietly."

"There's nothing quiet about war," General Hornworks pointed out, "once it gets cooking."

"That is the problem with you Westerners. You think sound and fury are the measurements of success. The greatest victories are silent ones. The Trojans knew this. Others did too."

"If you're looking for wooden horses," Hornworks said dryly, "we'd have to requisition a few."

"It has been done," said Chiun dismissively. "Are there other ways to destroy these missiles before they can be fired at us?"

"Sure. Hell, you can take out a Scud missile and launcher with a twenty-two rifle. Just shoot at the liquid-propellant stage. She'll blow right up and take the launcher with her. If there was a way to hit every missile at once, that little problem would be solved."

The hazel eyes of the Master of Sinanju narrowed.

"Where do the Kurds stand in this matter?" he asked thoughtfully.

"The Kurds—they're just a bunch of ragtag—"

Chiun held up a silencing hand. "Answer my question."

"Last I heard, they were forming irregular units—I mean legions. But my guess is that if conflict breaks out, the Kurds'll turn on the Iraitis durn quick."

Chiun nodded. "Then all that remains is to become acquainted with the mind of your enemy."

"We don't even know who's in charge up there, now that ol' Mad Ass is out of the picture."

"That villain is not dead. He lives. And it is his personality you must understand if you are to be triumphant over him. Now, you will study the papers I have provided you."

"What is this thing anyway?" General Hornworks wanted to know.

"It is your enemy's horoscope," said Chiun gravely. "I have cast it in Korean."

"That explains why I can't make it out," General Hornworks said dryly.

"I will teach you."

"Astrology?" General Hornworks asked in surprise.

"No. Korean."

General Winfield Scott Hornworks searched the wrinkled features of the old Oriental for signs of humor. Finding none, he drew in a deep breath and thought: Well, there goes the war.

# 14

President Razzik Azziz, AKA *al-Ze'em*, was growing desperate.

In power less than a day, he could feel his hold in his Revolting Command Council slipping with each passing hour. He wore a fresh uniform, and his upper lip was raw from its first encounter with a shaving blade in many years.

"What news?" he demanded, barging into the council room, where his subordinates sat around the table touching the unfamiliar nakedness under their noses.

"There is no answer from the Americans," reported the information minister. "Even the ambassador has abandoned the embassy."

He turned to the defense minister, his eyes pleading for good news.

"The American demons have taken their battle to the western outskirts of the city," the man reported.

"They are going away?" he asked, hope brightening his voice.

"It is impossible to say. But they have destroyed the entire western antimissile missile battery. Abominadad is now defenseless against an air attack."

"There is still our air force," the chief air-force general put in.

"Which will be decimated within two hours of a U.S.

first strike," said the Iraiti secretary of the navy, which was only slightly larger than the Irish navy.

No one disputed that. They all watched CNN, which had predicted this was inevitable, so they knew it was true.

Through the windows came an extended tortured crackling sound, like a thousand logs going through a car-crushing machine.

"What is that?" the president gasped, clutching the table edge.

The information minister went to a window.

"It is the royal Kurani roller coaster," he said. "It is being torn apart. They have climbed atop it and are battling furiously."

Taking up a pair of field glasses, the president went to the window.

He saw them clearly this time. Both the American who wore the purple and red of an Aladdin, and the nude blond American woman with more arms than were wholesome.

They were tearing off sections of track and using them as bludgeons. Each time a blow fell, the entire rickety roller coaster trembled like a precarious house of wooden matchsticks.

"Who is winning?" asked the foreign minister.

"It is as before," Azziz returned. "They are stalemated. Yet they seem tireless. What manner of beings could these be?"

No one had an answer to that.

Presently the defense minister had an idea.

"Perhaps there is a way to defeat them," he offered, his dark eyes alight.

The president lowered his field glasses. "Tell me."

"Gases. We will pour war gases down upon them."

"Will this work?"

"They have noses. They must breathe like mortals. If they breathe the gases in, they must die."

"Is it not dangerous to us?" wondered Azziz.

The defense minister shrugged unconcernedly. "The wind is from the east. The enemy are to the west. We may lose some of our western sector, but we will lose more than that if this madness continues unchecked."

The president considered only a moment. "Do it," he commanded.

Since the only missile battery in Abominadad had been decimated, the defense minister had to call the outpost of the Abaddon Air Base in order to effect a Scud strike.

"Yes, that is correct," he said. "I did say to launch your missiles at Abominadad. The western sector. The former Maddas City. You can do this?"

The defense minister listened. Absently he reached up to brush his mustache. Touching bare flesh, he felt a stab of fear. Then he remembered. It was safe to be without a mustache in Irait now that Maddas Hinsein was no more.

When the word came back that the missiles would soon be launched, the defense minister said, "Thank you," and lowered the phone to its cradle.

He heard the click just as the president shouted, "Wait! Do not launch!"

"Why not?"

"The wind has now shifted this way! In the name of Allah, call them back!"

Frantically the defense minister picked up the receiver. He began stabbing the keypad, his eyes starting from his head, his face sprouting a hot sheen of sweat.

Two rings later a bored voice said, "Achmed's Tyre Emporium."

This time true fear clutched at the defense minister's heart and would not let go. He stood there, his eyes stricken, the annoyed "Hello? Hello?" assaulting his unhearing ears through the trembling receiver.

"You have called it off?" shouted the president.

The defense minister hesitated, his tongue a cold slug

of fear in his dry mouth. Should be reveal that he had misdialed, or should he try again? With a new president it was impossible to tell which was the survivable option.

Then all choice fled the defense minister's mind.

From beyond the windows where the rest of the Revolting Command Council watched came a low roaring. It swelled to a screech, and at the apex of the sound came a steady *crump crump crump*.

Air-raid sirens wailed. From roofs all over Abominadad, antiaircraft artillery opened up, sending reddish-orange tracers streaking into the clear heavens.

The faces of the Revolting Command Council turned, eyes wide, mustacheless mouths forming identical bloodless lines. They regarded the defense minister with stupefied expressions.

Recognizing his predicament, the defense minister decided to lie.

"It was too late," he said miserably. "My loyal forces, eager to perform their sacred duty, could not wait to execute my order. It is done."

"So," said President Razzik Azziz thickly, "are we, brother Arabs. For all three missiles have missed. One has landed on this side of the Tigris. There are gases coming this way."

Then a gruff voice asked a deceptively innocuous question. It was the last voice any of them ever expected to hear again. It chilled their marrow as it asked:

"Where are all your mustaches?"

# 15

The voice repeated its harsh question: "Where are all your mustaches?"

As one, the right hands of the Revolting Command Council of the Republic of Irait flew to their naked, exposed upper lips.

"Which traitor among you is responsible for the disaster that has befallen our proud nation?" demanded the stern voice of Maddas Hinsein, Scimitar of the Arabs.

He stood in the doorway, flanked by blue-bereted Renaissance Guards. This evidence of their loyalty established without fear of contradiction, he waved them from the room. The door closed.

Fear roosted in each man's eyes. Paralysis gripped their very bones, as if their marrows had congealed.

In that moment's hesitation, Maddas roared, "I demand an answer!"

Deaf to the last dull *crump* coming through the window behind them, oblivious of the nerve-gas cloud that was lifting over the western skyline, the Revolting Command Council pointed at the current president of Irait, Razzik Azziz, who they realized was destined to go down in Iraiti history as the shortest-lived ruler since pre-Islamic days.

President Razzik Azziz realized this too. He pointed at the others.

"Precious Leader," Azziz said, sick-voiced. "They insisted I take your place. I told them, 'But no Arab could do that. It is preposterous.' They all refused the honor. Irait was in desperate straits. What could I do?"

Since the order to relax had not been given, the accusing fingers remained leveled. Arms trembled from nervous strain.

Maddas Hinsein, resplendent in a jet-black military uniform festooned with so much gold braid and green tinsel that he resembled a Christmas tree in mourning, put his hands on his thick hips.

"The hostages have been set free," he growled. "By whose orders?"

The fingers continued pointing.

Maddas nodded. "Our beloved capital has been gassed. By whom?"

The fingers stabbed the air anew. President Azziz switched hands.

Maddas nodded. "You have shaved your mustaches. Who allowed this?"

The fingers strained emphatically. Stiff features began melting like wax effigies.

Then President Razzik Azziz made the mistake that had cost more Iraiti officers their lives than enemy fire over the course of a decade of war with neighboring Irug. He attempted to reason with Maddas Hinsein.

"But, Precious Leader," he stuttered, "we thought you were dead. We shaved only to express our profound loss."

For a moment the fleshy brown face of Maddas Hinsein wavered in its scowl. His gruff features softened. A sudden moistness leapt into his calflike eyes.

"My brothers," he said, laying a hand over his massive chest. "You thought to honor me so? I am touched."

"We are glad you approve, Precious Leader," said President Razzik Azziz, lowering his aching arm.

It was then that Maddas Hinsein pulled his pearl-handled revolver and shot the man once in the belly.

Razzik Azziz was carried backward by a dumdum bullet that exerted over twelve thousand foot-pounds of velocity. It actually lifted him off his feet just before he slammed into the wall at his back.

He made a big red smear on the paint as he slowly slipped down to a sitting position, an uncomprehending expression on his freshly shaved face. As if radar-guided, dozen digits followed him down.

"The rest I could forgive," said Maddas Hinsein, stuffing his weapon back into his holster. "But only a fool would believe that the Scimitar of the Arabs was dead. Maddas Hinsein will die when he is ready, not before."

"We believed you were still alive," chorused the surviving Revolting Command Council members, their fingers still accusing the shuddering corpse that had been Razzik Azziz. "But he made us shave at gunpoint."

"Next time this happens, you will take the bullet in your brains before you lift a razor to your faces," ordered the Scimitar of the Arabs.

"As you command, O Precious Leader," they promised.

Maddas nodded. "Take your seats. We have work to do."

"But, the gas," sputtered the defense minister.

Maddas looked up sharply. "Is the window not closed?"

"Yes, Precious Leader."

"Then we have time."

And so, woodenly, they took their seats around the rectangular table, which had a huge hole cut in the center. Maddas Hinsein had decreed it be built that way so no assassin could lurk under his meeting table and strike him dead. Also, so there was no place to hide from his wrath.

# 16

An orbiting KH-12 satellite first detected the impact craters mushrooming along the western section of Abominadad, and the resulting eruption of gas.

High-resolution images were down-linked to a top-secret CIA ground station in Nurrungar Valley, Australia, from there microwaved to the Washington, D.C. and the National Photo Intelligence Center for processing, and passed on to CIA analysts in Langley, Virgina.

A preliminary analysis revealed that the impact craters were caused by Scud missiles, launched from mobile erector launchers. This puzzled CIA analysts. The only Scuds deployed in what the Pentagon had dubbed the Iraiti-Kuran Theater of Operations were in Irait and Syria. A Syrian strike on Irait seemed improbable.

Then the spectroscopic analysis of the clouds came in.

"Sarin?" said the chief analyst in a puzzled voice. "Only the Iraitis have Sarin." Then the significance of his discovery reached him.

Down in the Tank—the nukeproof basement strategy room of the Pentagon—the chairman of the Joint Chiefs of Staff accepted the telexed CIA report, read it grimly, and turned to the remaining officers in the room.

"Bad news. We have confirmation that the Iraitis have definitely refitted their Scuds to deliver war gas."

"How do we know this?" asked the chief of naval operations, who had visions of unleashing a few Trident and Polaris missiles on Abominadad in a massive preemptive strike destined to go down in naval history and incidentally put him in the running for the 1992 presidential elections.

The chairman's clipped answer dashed his hopes like seawater washing over a cutter's bow.

"They just hit their own capital," he said. "Took out their entire defensive missile batteries and one of the largest roller coasters known to man."

This impressed everyone. No one had ever heard of a successful air strike on a roller coaster.

"Civil war?" asked the Army Chief of Staff.

The chairman strode over to a telephone, saying, "No idea. I'd better inform the President about this. It sounds big."

The President of the United States didn't know if civil war had broken out in Irait. But he had hopes. It would be the solution to all his problems. Up to this moment he had been praying for an earthquake.

After he hung up from the Pentagon, he called the CIA. They had no information either.

All the hostages had come out of Abominadad. So had the U.S. ambassador and his staff. They were blacked out, intelligence-wise.

The only missing factor was the whereabouts of Reverend Juniper Jackman and anchorman Don Cooder. They had not come out with the others. Only days ago the President had been prepared to go to war over their execution. But with the death of Maddas Hinsein, the American public—and more important, the media, which had been stoking the war fires—had turned their attention to the overriding question: was Armageddon near?

The President got out of his Oval Office chair and went over to the window overlooking the Rose Garden.

The solid pine flooring under his feet felt uncertain, almost rubbery. Outside his door, a Secret Service guard stood clutching a green canvas sack that contained a gas mask emblazoned with the Presidential Seal. As a counterterrorist precaution, Jersey barriers ringed every significant Washington building from the White House to the Lincoln Memorial. It was as if, he thought, he and the world stood on the crumbling edge of a great abyss.

He wondered why he thought of an abyss. Outside, beyond the latticework of glass panes, the sun shone and the roses were dewed from a brief morning shower. The world as seen from the White House looked postcard perfect.

So why did he feel like the lead lemming closing in on a precipice, and not leader of the greatest nation on earth?

# 17

General Winfield Scott Hornworks burst into the basement war room of the Star in the Center of the Flower of the East Military Base, waving a telex flash message.

"I got bodacious news," he crowed. "The damn Iraitis are cleaning their own plow for us!"

Seated around the floor, on reed mats, Master Chiun, Prince General Bazzaz and Sheik Fareem looked up from huddled consultation. Their faces quirked into annoyed expressions.

"Speak English," requested Chiun.

"I *am* speaking English," Hornworks insisted. "Some hotshot Iraiti rocket unit—I mean legion—has up and wiped out the Abominadad air-defense ring all by his lonesome, including a roller coaster they were using as an antimissile shield. It's probably a coup. Maybe civil war."

The annoyed expressions fled, leaving in their places identical stony ones.

"Don't you get it?" Hornworks snapped. "It's practically victory."

"It is nothing," said Chiun flatly. "Come and sit. We have much to discuss."

"Well, pardon me all to hell," muttered the general. "I thought we might all take some comfort from the collapse of the enemy."

Unhappily, General Hornworks lowered his burly body onto a mat. He waved the telex under their noses. "At least read this thing. It's from the Pentagon. The Iraitis have gassed themselves."

Chiun accepted the sheet, glanced over it briefly, and threw it high into the air. Slipping and sliding down the air currents, it was reduced to confetti under a sudden flurrying of his long fingernails.

"That was an official communiqué," Hornworks said dispiritedly.

"And this is a war council," said Chiun gravely. "We have made our decision."

"What decision?"

"The decision to go to war, of course."

"War? We don't need to go to war no more. You haven't been listening, have you? The Iraitis are at war with their own dang selves. All we gotta do is sit tight and pick up the pieces when they stop falling."

"And you have forgotten your horoscopic lessons? The tyrant Maddas will not be stopped by mere civil war. He will emerge victorious to vex us anew. We must be ready to strike before this happens."

"The Master of Sinanju speaks truly," said Sheik Fareem in a grave voice.

"*Inshallah,*" said Prince General Bazzaz.

"We can't go to war without presidential authorization," said General Hornworks in a sullen voice, not caring one whit whether Mars was ascendant over Saturn or not.

"I am the ruler of Hamidi Arabia," said the sheik. "If the Master of Sinanju says that war is necessary to defeat the aggressor, then there will be war and you will be silent."

"I can't believe I'm hearing this," moaned Hornworks, burying his face in his hands. "I'm a West Point graduate. I'm the ninth Hornworks to rise to a generalship in the U.S. Army."

"I have decided to promote you," came the voice of Chiun.

Hornworks looked up, haggard and blinking.

"Promote! To what? I'm a four-star general."

"You are now Praetor Hornworks," answered the Master of Sinanju.

"*Pray* . . . what?"

"It is what you would call second in command," explained Prince General Bazzaz.

"That's a goldurn demotion!" Hornworks exploded. "I'm supreme allied commander, CentCom! You can't demote me!"

"We will fight as the Romans did," added Chiun, ignoring the outburst.

"That's gonna be kinda hard," Hornworks snorted. "To the best of my recollection, the Romans didn't have much of an air force."

"And we shall have none," said Chiun flatly.

"How're we gonna win a war without an air force?" Hornworks exploded.

"By superior strategy. First, you will reorganize your legions."

"I already got them redeployed according to that dang turtle shell."

"It is a tortoiseshell, and your enemy already knows how you are to fight this war," Chiun corrected.

"Yeah. By massive air strikes."

"Exactly why you will not do this."

"We can't get into a bloody ground slog!"

"You will not. First, you must select sixty of your bravest centurions—"

"Centurions? Is that kinda like a captain?"

"Possibly," Chiun said vaguely. "Each centurion will command a century of one hundred infantry. Six centuries will comprise a cohort."

"Companies and battalions," said General Hornworks, beginning to write this down. Since he no longer had his telex, he used his sleeve. "Yeah, yeah. My military history is coming back to me now. A division is what—a legion? We already got a sackful of legionnaires—all French."

"Then your horsemen."

Hornworks looked up from his sleeve. "We don't have any durn horsemen."

"What do you call the iron turtles with the long noses?"

"Tanks. Oh, you mean tank cavalry?"

"Yes. The equities. You will prepare them to enter the land now called Kuran."

"We send in the tanks without air cover and we're sunk," Hornworks snorted.

"There will be no air cover," pronounced the Master of Sinanju.

Pain on his face, General Hornworks looked to the others for support.

"There will be no air cover," said Sheik Fareem.

"There will be no air cover," added Prince General Bazzaz.

"Whose side are you on, anyway?" Hornworks growled.

"The winning side," Bazzaz told him.

Hornworks winced. "What about naval support? Navy gunnery is the finest in the world—much as I'm loath to admit it as a career army officer."

Chiun fingered his beard. "The Romans had no navy. Navies are Greek." He shook his bald head. "No, we will have no navy. You may send the ships away. The Mesopotamians once fought the Greeks, and would be prepared for such obvious tactics. They never fought the Romans. The advantage would be ours."

"Advantage? You're setting us up for the greatest defeat in the history of warfare!"

"Only if you fail to carry out the instructions of the imperator."

"What's an imperator?"

"I am."

"Is that kinda like a general?" Hornworks wondered.

"It is absolutely like a general," Chiun told him.

"Figures," Hornworks said morosely.

"What am I?" asked Prince General Bazzaz with a straight face.

"You are now prince imperator," Chiun told him.

"Prince Imperator Bazzaz." The prince turned to the sheik. "Does that not sound wonderful, Father?"

The old sheik beamed. "I am proud of you, my son."

"Since navies are Greek and everyone knows the Greeks are unrepentant pork-eaters," Bazzaz said firmly, "I withdraw my request for a personal aircraft carrier."

"Done. What would you have in its place?"

"My very own legion," Bazzaz said quickly.

"Since this request befits a prince imperator, I will agree to this," Sheik Fareem said, clapping his hands once.

"I hate to break into this touching family scene," said General Hornworks, "but I'd like to point out that what we're discussing here is sending all our forward units into the biggest breastworks of entrenched positions and high-density troop concentrations since World War One."

"Yes," said Chiun. "That is what we're talking about here."

"These front-line units, they're mostly kids and old men," Hornworks added. "They're keeping their elite Renaissance Guard in the rear."

The Master of Sinanju nodded. "That is my understanding."

"Our people will be chopped up before we even get to the elite uni . . . centuries. Assuming we get that far. Once they realize we're not gonna use air and sea power, they're gonna hit us with their missiles. If they don't get the drop on us while we're all sitting on our duffs brushing up on our Latin."

"They will use their missiles first," Chiun decided. "It will be up to our *socii* to deal with those. Our allies."

"How? Sneak a British SAS team into Irait? We start blowing them up with twenty-twos, and they'll just launch the rest of them."

"We will not do it that way."

"Yeah, how we gonna do it? By magic?"

"That is why I have summoned you here, Praetor Hornworks," Chiun said. "I must have a method of rendering these devices harmless. It must be a silent method. It cannot be complicated because the *socii* I envision to undertake this action are not trained to work with complicated tools. Stealth will be their chief virtue."

"Stealth!" cried Praetor Hornworks. "Now you're talking! The Fifty-seventh Tactical Air Wing is standing ready to carpet-bomb the bejesus out of those heathens—in a manner of speaking."

"Send them home," said Chiun indignantly. "We will drop no booms, fire no cannon, and destroy no carpets. These primitive methods are not the way of Imperator Chiun. We will defeat the enemy with our brains."

"Let me get this straight—you want a way that will knock out those missile launchers so that no one will know they're knocked out?" Hornworks asked in a dubious tone.

"Yes."

"But that's impossible."

"Nonsense," said the sheik. "You are an American. Americans are very ingenious. The world knows this."

Prince Imperator Bazzaz nodded eagerly. "Yes, everyone knows Americans are ingenious. Your movies are beyond compare. You create the most wonderful toys, like aircraft carriers. Surely you have a big wondrous toy to make this happen?"

Praetor Winfield Scott Hornworks' eyes traveled from face to face around the war room.

"Why do I get the feeling I'm just a spear-carrier in this comic opera?" he grumbled.

"Because you are," said the Master of Sinanju simply.

# 18

President Maddas Hinsein paused to light up a Cuban cigar with a cylindrical pipe lighter that emitted a blue flame almost a foot long. He took his time, rolling the clipped tip of the cigar in the flame, watching it darken and shrivel. Presently it caught like a slow coal. He collapsed the lighter, cutting off the high blue flame.

The lighter went into a pocket and the cigar went into his mouth. He puffed thoughtfully while, beyond the window which, of those in the council room, only he faced squarely, the noxious yellow cloud of Sarin nerve gas rolled inexorably toward the Palace of Sorrows. The nervous antiaircraft fire had died down to an occasional colorful sputter.

Those sitting on either side of the long open meeting table were very aware of that window. Their eyes careened toward it often, only to be drawn inexorably back toward the too-calm figure of their leader.

Once the cigar was really going, Maddas Hinsein drew in a double lungful of aromatic tobacco smoke. His barrel chest swelled. He held the smoke deep within him.

Then, in a steady insolent stream, he released the smoke. It rolled down the long table, a bluish-gray harbinger of the death that would soon be theirs.

Everyone held his breath. To inhale the expensive

tobacco smoke that had emerged from the Precious One's lungs was a transgression punishable by hanging.

"Go ahead," prompted Maddas Hinsein, "inhale. I do not mind. It is good smoke. And you have earned it, loyal ones."

Obediently the Revolting Command Council leaned into the rolling smoke, inhaling greedily. They recoiled, coughing and hacking. The stuff was wretched—worse than the nerve gas could ever be. Or so they imagined.

"The Arab who can inhale this heady smoke and not cough is the man who may succeed me one day," Maddas Hinsein said with a careless gesture. "When I am prepared to ascend into Paradise," he added.

"Precious Leader," said the foreign minister, "if we do not evacuate this building soon, we will all be dead from our own war gas."

"That is the beauty of our position," said Maddas Hinsein coolly.

"What is?"

Maddas Hinsein took the cigar from his mouth and bestowed upon his council a broad, toothy smile. "We are already dead. Therefore we are capable of anything—any valor, any grand gesture."

And he opened his smiling mouth to give vent to a low, humorless laughter. It sounded like something a mechanical carnival clown might utter. There was nothing human in it.

The Revolting Command Council had no choice. They joined in. Not to laugh was to die, and even though to stay in the palace meeting room was to die also, they unanimously preferred to die by gas than at the hands of the man they called Precious Leader.

"Brief me," Hinsein commanded, going instantly somber. He flicked cigar ash into the hole in the table, as if it were some great ashtray.

"The Americans have not attacked," the defense minister reported. "Their aircraft no longer fly. In fact, they are sending their carrier battle groups into open sea. We do not know why."

"They have not attacked because they fear our gases," Maddas pronounced. "Therefore, they will never attack. We are safe forever from the Americans."

Everyone knew that this was a colossal miscalculation.

"Then it was good that the former defense minister released the hostages," the defense minister suggested carefully.

Maddas frowned darkly. "He was a fool. But Irait will survive his foolishness. For deep in the dungeons below us, we have two of the most important hostages anyway."

The council leaned toward their leader. "Precious Leader?" one muttered.

"I refer to the infidel black priest Jackman and the television reader Don Cooder."

At that, every man at the table paled under the caramel coloring of his Arab complexion.

"They are our insurance against further American aggression," added Maddas Hinsein.

"But you just said that the Americans will not attack," the foreign minister stuttered.

"They will not," Maddas said flatly. "But they may wish to after we enter the next phase of our annexation of Greater Arabia."

Around the table, jaws dropped. "Precious Leader?"

Maddas paused to draw on his smoldering cigar. "We are going to take Hamidi Arabia," he said with quiet confidence.

Jaws clicked shut. Silence filled the room. All thought of the approaching nerve gas fled. A tiny gurgle broke the silence. It was followed by another. Those whose bladders still held reached down to their laps to prevent their gall from joining that of their comrades on the floor.

"But . . . how?" This was from the defense minister,

who would have to execute the operation—or be executed for refusing a direct order.

"By striking at the most vulnerable point of the infidel army of occupation," said Maddas Hinsein, as if suggesting a stroll along the banks of the Tigris.

"Can we do that with impunity?" wondered the education minister.

President Hinsein nodded. "Yes. Once the world understands as you do that Maddas Hinsein still lives—and that the most important of our foreign guests do as well."

"You propose a news conference, Precious Leader?"

"I do."

"Do you propose this soon?" he asked, eyes flicking to the window and the hazy mustard-colored sky beyond it.

Maddas nodded confidently.

"Then let me suggest that we conduct this conference down in the gasproof dungeon of this very palace."

Maddas wrinkled his nose. Outside the window, the yellow gas rolled closer. He placed his fingertips against his cheek in a thoughtful manner, as if reconsidering.

"To run from our own gas could be seen as a sign of weakness," he pointed out.

Every man in the room held his breath. For one reason or another.

When their Precious Leader at last spoke, they released it with closed eyes and muttered prayers to benevolent Allah.

"But it would be the last thing they would expect from brave Arabs such as we," decided Maddas Hinsein, smiling faintly.

"Then let us do this immediately," cried the information minister, pounding the table with his fist. "Why should we delay? The Americans must know we are not to be trifled with."

"Yes, we will go now," said the Scimitar of the Arabs as he stood up.

They let him go first. The Renaissance Guardsmen who had been standing sentry outside fell in behind him. There would be no opportunity to stab this madman in the back, they realized. It made them wish to weep.

The elevator ride to the dungeon took an eternity. No one could remember it having taken so long in the past. Their faces were a smoky lavender from holding in their breaths. All except Maddas Hinsein, who continued to breathe normally.

He was funny that way.

# 19

Samdup watched a snow owl swoop into the valley and felt in his heart a sharp pang of hunger for the same boundless freedom the wild bird enjoyed.

Samdup was a Tibetan. No Tibetan was free, or had been since the Chinese People's Liberation Army had stormed in, killing the lamas, burning down the beautiful temples, and turning a land of peace into an outpost of barbarism. That was long ago.

Samdup was neither priest nor soldier. He was too young to remember the days of the gentle Dalai Lama, who once had exerted his benevolence over the mountain kingdom. The greatest destruction had occured before Samdup was born. The Tibet he knew was but a shadow of what it had been. So said the elders, whom Samdup revered.

The snow owl shook its dappled wings majestically, alighting on a high crag of snow and rock. When it seemed that it would not take wing soon, Samdup resumed his journey.

The high peaks of the Himalayas were quiet, with a lack of sound that a non-Tibetan would term loud. To a native, the mountains always expressed the silence in loud voices. It was a paradox, and imponderable. But it was pure Tibet.

So when strange sounds made the mountains ring like great gongs of brass, Samdup froze in his tracks.

The sound seemed to come from the east, moving west. It was a thunder of a sound. It began as a rumble. It continued as a rumble. A rolling, unending rumble. An eternal rumble.

And inextricable from that extended sound was another. It might have been the product of a thousand benevolent gods singing in chorus. The rising sun could conceivably author such a song, had the sun a throat. Beautiful maidens might produce such sounds, had they low, yet melodic voices.

It reminded Samdup of the lamas, whose surviving members sometimes congregated in the potala—the great temple of Lamism—to chant and pray to benevolent Buddha.

But this sound was so loud, so wondrous, that no ordinary lama brought it forth into the world, he knew.

It could mean only one thing, thought Samdup, his heart quickening. It was the song that heralded the return of the Dalai Lama.

Breaking into a run, Samdup ran to meet it.

After twenty minutes he was forced to slow to a walk. But it was a brisk walk, for his heart leapt high, his feet feeling as if they were encased in jade shoes.

The Dalai Lama had returned, and Samdup would be the first to greet him!

After many minutes of walking, a PLA truck column came up the road and roared past him, faces joyless.

Samdup stepped out of the way.

"Where are you going?" he shouted after them.

A young soldier only a few years older than he shouted back, "To defeat the aggressor."

And Samdup's brisk stride faltered. His wide peaceful face grew as dull as a weather-beaten gong. Tears started in a corner of one eye.

The Dalai Lama had come back only to fall before the godless Chinese barbarians, thought Samdup.

Still, it was a moment of high drama. Samdup quickened his pace. He must behold it. If only to tell the world of Chinese cruelty.

Only minutes later, the truck column roared toward him, in full retreat.

The looks of horror etched in the survivors' faces were shocking. The wounded were many. They lay about the back of the trucks like smashed dolls in green uniforms. Their eyes told of an encounter with a power greater than mortal man.

Samdup raced on, his heart straining as if to burst. Wild tears of joy streamed down his apple cheeks.

The Dalai Lama had returned in triumph! Not even the wicked Chinese had been able to turn him from the path of right.

On and on ran Samdup the Tibetan.

The thunder swelled and the song of the mightiest lama continued its bountiful ululations. Nothing so beautiful had ever been heard on earth, Samdup thought.

Soon he rounded a snow-dusted hillock, and there the road stretched out as straight as the spokes on a prayer wheel.

At first there was only dust. It swirled and roiled and was impenetrable to sight.

This was as it should be, Samdup thought. The coming of the Dalai Lama was too great a sight not to be obscured from men.

Samdup took a position in the center of the road and bowed twice. He stuck his tongue out as far as he could. This was the proper manner of greeting among Tibetans. He showed a good long length of tongue, did Samdup the Tibetan.

And through the swirling dust, a dark shape emerged. Mighty flanks rippled with unstoppable muscularity. A thousand remorseless eyes seemed to wink like stars that had hardened to black diamonds. And hooves of horn unlike anything Samdup had ever imagined could be discerned dimly.

And through it all, the song swelled until it filled Samdup's very soul.

He fell to his knees before the sheer grace of it all.

He was found in the center of the road two days later, stamped as flat as a dog under a PLA tank's tracks. No one could explain what had happened to him, and so his body was thrown to the dogs, as was the custom with the honored dead. The lamas prayed for his soul, and hoped that he had not suffered.

In truth, Samdup had died with his heart full of joy.

The quiet thunder continued to roll west.

# 20

Don Cooder was angry. Really angry. He had not been so angry since the network had hired that Korean barracuda Cheeta Ching as weekend anchor. He wouldn't have minded a crack reporter in the slot. It would have been good contrast. But there was no way he could compete with hair like hers. Next contact, he vowed, he would have a best-hair clause written in.

"This is an outrage," he stormed, pacing the ill-lit dungeon room. "Who does Maddas think he is—William Paley reincarnated? I'm not just any old hostage. I'm the highest-paid anchorman in the universe. Even people who never watched me are in awe of Don Cooder. I get more respect that Superman."

"Superman gets higher ratings and he's in reruns," put in Reverend Jackman sourly. "Maybe you should wear one of *his* sweaters."

Cooder shook a fist at the dripping walls. "Last time, I got a hotel room. Clean sheets. Room service. All the proper amenities."

"You got them because you were with me. Don't kid yourself."

"No way. Maddas is a Moslem. He's not kowtowing to you, a Baptist minister. Hell, those people talk about the Crusades like they happened last Tuesday." Don Cooder shook his wildly disheveled black hair. "No, you were treated good because they mistook you for my friend."

"So explain how we ended up in this fix."

Don Cooder stopped pacing. He rubbed his blue-bestubbled jaw, bringing the bags under his eyes into sharp relief. He drove a fist into one palm, producing a meaty smack.

"It's fate. I was destined to be the world's witness to Maddas Hinsein's resurrection. I'd strangle puppies for a camcorder and a satellite uplink right about now. The greatest story in the world. And I can't broadcast it. I'll bet that sticky-haired Cheeta Ching has got my dressing room by now."

"She can have it. I want to get out of this heckhole alive."

"They won't kill us," Don Cooder said stubbornly. "I'm too famous."

"You got a short memory, gloryhound. They already tried to execute us once. We got a reprieve, is all."

"Nonsense. That was obviously staged so that Maddas could disappear."

"The man who believes that has got a major crush on Tinkerbell too," scoffed Reverend Jackman. "I told you not to tip Maddas when he brought us to the palace like that. It was an insult. Man's a head of state."

"I always tip cabdrivers, no matter what," Don Cooder returned. "They start wailing on me when I don't."

The drumbeat of footsteps filtered through the rusty iron bars embedded in the heavy oaken door.

"Someone's coming," Reverend Jackman muttered, his eyes going so wide they looked close to dropping from their sockets.

"Do you wanna check, or shall I?" Cooder muttered.

"You're by the door."

"Yeah, but I'm not sure I'm going to like what I see."

In the end, both men went to the bars.

Heads butting, they vied for a good look.

"It's Maddas Hinsein," Jackman hissed when it was his turn.

Don Cooder shoved him aside. His mouth went slack.

"And he's got a whole bunch of guards with him."

"Do they look like the kind who came for us last time?"

"Why?"

"Because if they're here to stand us before a firing squad, I'd kinda like a little advance notice."

"I can't tell," Cooder admitted.

"Why not?"

"I'm afraid to open my eyes," said Don Cooder.

Reverend Jackman pushed Don Cooder aside.

"Looks kinda like an execution squad to me," he said dully.

That opened Don Cooder's eyes. They went sick.

"I guess this is where we separate the men from the boys," he intoned. "I guess this is the end of the line. The final roundup. The last sign-off. The—"

"I'm gonna slap you if you go all hysterical on me," Reverend Jackman warned.

Then the footsteps were right outside the door and both men shrank back from the sound of a brass key grating in a rusty lock.

The ponderous door creaked open, filling the dungeon room with a wavering light from ranked wall torches.

Maddas Hinsein was the first to enter. He entered smiling. Somehow that smile made the blood run in their veins like Freon.

"He's showing his teeth," whispered Don Cooder.

"You think it's a smile?" asked Reverend Jackman.

"Well, he doesn't look all that hungry."

"Okay, he's smiling. Is that good news or bad?"

"Well, I did tip him double, even though we wanted the airport."

Reverend Jackman frowned. "Somehow I don't think that's why he's smiling."

The information minister slipped into the room. He was not smiling. In fact, he looked like a man who had just dodged a locomotive and was trying to regain his nerve.

"I bid you greetings from his excellency President Maddas Hinsein of Irait," the man said in a voice he tried to make portentous, but which came out tinny.

"Ask his most gracious excellency if he will agree to an interview," Don Cooder said quickly. "I can promise him global news coverage."

"Our Precious Leader requests that we both join him in a press conference."

"Press conference? I'm not good at those. A two-shot would be better. You savvy two-shot? One on one?"

"Our Precious Leader wishes that you both inform the world of his miraculous escape from a foolish assassination attempt."

"Glad to," said Reverend Jackman, stepping forward. "Just point the way. I'm ready."

"Who invited you?" snarled Don Cooder, stepping between the reverend and the president.

Reverend Jackman pointed toward Maddas Hinsein, who although he did not understand English, seemed to be enjoying the sight of their bickering with immense relish.

"He did," said Reverend Jackman. "You got a complaint, take it up with my main man there."

Don Cooder did, although indirectly. "Could you ask his most royal highness why he's holding his press conference?" he inquired of the information minister.

"Our Precious Leader begs to inform you that you will assist him in announcing his ultimatum to the infidel occupation forces in Hamidi Arabia," the information minister explained.

"Why do you need us?" blurted Reverend Jackman.

The question was conveyed to Maddas Hinsein in Arabic.

Upon receiving the answer, the information minister turned as pale as a burnoose. He was so flustered he made his protest in English, which his president did not understand.

"But, Precious Leader," he said, "how can you offer him the post of information minister? I am your loyal information minister."

"No way I'm settling for information minister," Reverend Jackman said indignantly. "It's the vice-presidency or nothing."

"What's the salary?" asked Don Cooder.

Before another word could be spoken, President Maddas Hinsein drew his pearl-handled revolver and shot his information minister dead in mid-protest.

His corpse fell across the shoes of Don Cooder and Reverend Juniper Jackman. Neither man moved.

Another council member stepped forward.

"Our Precious Leader has decreed that due to unforeseen losses among the Revolting Command Council," he said stiffly, "you, Cooder, and you, Jackman, have been offered the positions of information minister and vice-president respectively. Do you accept?"

Reverend Juniper Jackman and Don Cooder blinked. Slowly their heads turned toward one another. Their eyes met. Their mouths opened. They looked down at the twitchy corpse of the late Iraiti information minister, who looked back at them with eyes that did not see.

Their gaze jerked up to meet that of Maddas Hinsein, Scimitar of the Arabs.

"We—" Reverend Jackman started to say.

"—gladly accept," Don Cooder finished.

"Amen."

"Make that a *salaam*," Don Cooder said hastily. "No offense, *effendi. Wallah!*" He smiled weakly and threw in a loyal salute.

# 21

Harold W. Smith happened to be home when the surprise telecast was satellited out of Abominadad. He was watching a National Geographic special on peeptoad migration in Rhode Island. It was so dull that his wife, Maude, had gone to bed ten minutes into the program. After the beaming features of Maddas Hinsein resolved on the screen, Smith was grateful for that minor blessing.

A mordant voice-over said, "This is Television Abominadad, broadcasting the glorious news that our Precious Leader Maddas Hinsein the First has reclaimed primacy over the ancient capital, soon to be the capital of Greater Arabia."

"My God," gasped Smith. "Chiun was correct."

The camera pulled back, showing Maddas Hinsein, one arm raised in a characteristic messianic gesture, standing on a balcony of the Palace of Sorrows. Below, a clapping crowd surged.

Maddas wore a white burnoose and flowing *ghurta*. He looked like a fat glowworm with a caramel-coated face.

"These pictures were taken early today, showing our precious leader bestowing his blessings on the people of Abominadad, who had just survived a cruel gas attack by criminal U.S. forces," the mordant voice went on in English as thick as blood pudding.

Smith started. "Gas attack? Impossible!"

"In a twist of kismet, the gas killed few Arabs but completely extinguished the lives of two foreign agents allied with the American imperialists," ran the mordant voice-over.

Another voice—Smith recognized it as belonging to BCN network anchorwoman Cheeta Ching—broke in to explain, "This transmission is coming to you live from Abominadad, Irait. Due to the importance of the Gulf crisis, BCN has elected to break programming at this time. A full wrap-up will follow, along with a late update on my heroic struggle to become impregnated."

The picture switched, showing two bodies in the rubble. One was of a young blond woman lying facedown. The fact that she had an extra set of arms was not obvious, but neither was it entirely hidden to viewers. Her skin was as black as coal tar—a certain symptom of nerve-gas poisoning. The camera panned over to another body, and Harold Smith saw a familiar face, one that had been beamed out of Irait once before.

The face of America's secret weapon, Remo Williams.

Remo lay on his back, attired in a torn profusion of purple and scarlet silks. His eyes were open, his mouth twisted. He neither moved nor seemed to see.

The panic that seized Smith's vitals at this latest exposure of CURE's enforcement arm subsided when he realized that Remo was clearly dead. His head lay at a crazy angle, indicating a broken neck. His throat was a livid purplish blue, like a great bruise. His skin, too, was the color of slate.

The picture went dark. Then the screen framed a podium on which the Revolting Command Council sat, attired in frog-green military uniforms. Smith frowned. They wore their military attire only when they were about to threaten some one.

Baroque martial music blared.

Abruptly the council members jumped to their feet

and burst into applause. The light illuminated their mustaches. They looked odd and flat, as if painted on.

The camera swung around, catching Maddas Hinsein, a towering figure in a gold-and-white uniform and black beret, as he swaggered into the room.

On either side of him, looking for all the world like the condemned, walked Reverend Juniper Jackman and Don Cooder.

"My God!" Smith croaked.

Smith always kept his worn briefcase beside him. He reached for this now. Throwing the disarming latches, he lifted the lid to reveal a mini-computer and a portable telephone hookup. Smith stabbed a button that tied it into the dedicated line to the White House.

It took several rings, but the President of the United States finally answered, out of breath.

"Smith. Do you see what I see?"

"I am afraid so," Smith replied tightly. Like twin camera lenses, his gray eyes were focused at the flickering TV images.

The camera tracked the unlikely trio as they took their seats at the table, Jackman and Cooder settling on either side of the president of Irait. They looked like food tasters at the inaugural banquet of an extremely unpopular king.

"And now," the heavily accented announcer said, "his glorious excellency the Scimitar of the Arabs, President Maddas Hinsein."

Maddas Hinsein began reading from a sheet of paper. He read slowly, in a low, sonorous voice. Every word was in Arabic.

Smith held the phone to his chest, waiting for the usual English translation, but none was forthcoming. He assumed there was a problem with the audio.

The insistent buzz of the President's voice coming from the buried receiver forced Harold Smith to lift the earpiece to his own ear.

"What the heck is he saying?" the President wanted to know.

"I cannot say, Mr. President," Smith replied. "But Maddas Hinsein is extremely calculating. This is designed to play to an Arabic-speaking audience, and I suspect the presence of Jackman and Cooder is meant to warn us against interference."

"You think he's trying to break up the UN coalition?"

"It is possible," Smith admitted.

"And what was that stuff about a U.S. gas attack? We know his own people gassed Abominadad."

"This may be a propaganda position, possibly a pretext for whatever he plans next."

"But what the heck *is* he planning?"

"I do not know," said Harold W. Smith, who strained with his free ear to catch everything being said by Maddas Hinsein, despite his almost complete inability to comprehend the Arabic language.

# 22

Yussef Zarzour would have given his right eye to have listened to the very important speech being given by President Maddas Hinsein over the Iraiti airwaves.

But as a colonel in the Renaissance Guard, he had his patriotic duty to perform.

The orders had come by radio from the Precious Leader himself.

"Take your Scud launcher to the Maddas Line," President Hinsein had instructed.

The Maddas Line was a Maginot Line of earthen-berm fortifications and barbed-wire coils just above the Kuran-Hamidi Arabian border. When the UN forces attacked, as surely they would, they would have to breach that horrendous fortified barrier.

"Park it at Launch Station Ibn Khaldoon," Maddas added.

"At once, Precious Leader," Colonel Zarzour said, saluting snappily, even though he was communicating by field radio. Who knew but that there might be a spy for the president lurking nearby? So it was better to salute and keep one's head than not to and risk losing it.

"When you are there, set your missile for coordinate 334."

"Three-three-four. Yes, yes, I have it."

"Then contact me. Personally."

Leaping into the driver's booth of the eight-wheeled mobile erector-launcher, Colonel Zarzour drove it out of its sand-colored protective revetment.

He had driven madly. The launcher barreled south through the featureless talcum-powder-like sands, resembling a giant camel-colored lipstick container on wheels.

When he ran out of petrol—petrol being a precious commodity during the crisis, thanks to the anti-Irait embargo—some forty kilometers south of Station Khaldoon, Zarzour faced a choice. Commit suicide or lie boldly.

He decided to lie, not boldly, but brazenly. If he shirked his duty, the Scimitar of the Arabs would have his body interred with dead pigs as punishment for his dereliction. There were worse fates than suicide, and Maddas Hinsein had compiled a list of them, which he sometimes read aloud on Iraiti television as a kind of poem to loyalty. He was not sometimes called the Scourge of the Arabs because he was unafraid to scourge the Arabs as well as the infidel unbelievers.

"Precious Leader," Colonel Zarzour reported by radio, "I am at the appointed place."

"Good. Launch."

It was not the order Zarzour had expected. He had not been sure what to expect.

But because he did not want to spend eternity with the corrupt flesh of unclean animals, he went to the control panel and initiated the launch sequence.

The missile canister reared up with the whine of toiling machinery, until it was completely vertical. Colonel Zarzour punched in the targeting coordinates.

Then, tears in his eyes because he knew these coordinates were in Hamidi Arabia, a land of fellow Moslems, Zarzour initiated the firing sequence. Then he ran for his life.

Dense black smoke began generating at the base of the missile. The stern vomited an orange tail of flame and thundered straight up. The desert air quaked and vibrated.

When the Soviet Union first sold Irait their top-of-the-line Scud missile system back in the days when the two nations were allies, they did so with complete confidence that even if Maddas Hinsein should acquire a nuclear and chemical warfare capability and undertake some grandiose misadventure, the Scuds would avail him little because they were notoriously unreliable.

The Scud missile that lifted off from Launch Station Ibn Khaldoon, turning south, should have been no different. But through a quirk of Soviet technology, and the fact that it had been fired from the wrong position, its gyroscopic inertial guidance system, shifting and compensating in confusion, did something no Scud had ever before done in the history of modern warfare.

It struck its assigned target. Dead center.

# 23

Praetor Winfield Scott Hornworks got the call in the privacy of his air-conditioned office.

He blanched at the sound of the anxious voice buzzing in his ear. "Oh, no. Oh, no," he moaned. His voice trailed off into a kind of sick mew.

Woodenly he replaced the tactical field telephone receiver when the voice was through reporting. A man learning that he had terminal cancer might wear such an expression.

Taking up his non-issue ostrich-plume helmet, he trudged out of the office and down to the basement war room, where Imperator Chiun and Prince Imperator Bazzaz were examining flash messages.

"It's over," Hornworks said leadenly.

Sheik Fareem looked up. "What is, Praetor Hornworks?"

"The war," the American general said in a crestfallen tone. "It's done with. We lost."

"How can this be?" demanded Chiun, Master of Sinanju.

"The Iraitis hit us where we really live. Our army's sunk. We've suffered complete tactical paralysis. We're talking about the worst military defeat since the Little Big Horn."

"Speak English."

"They got the 324th Data Processing Cohort," Praetor Hornworks explained, dejection muting his voice. "It was a Scud, damn their eyes. Warhead filled with nerve gas. The poor bastards—I mean bastards *and* bitches, since we're coed now—never had a chance. Every one of 'em's down."

"How many dead?" asked Chiun, his eyes pained.

"None. They got into their chemical suits just in time. They're sick as dogs, but they'll pull through, once we're done medevacking them to Germany."

"Can these worthy ones be replaced?" asked Imperator Chiun.

"You kidding me?" Praetor Hornworks said indignantly. "You know how long it takes to train a soldier in VMS? Besides, that ain't our biggest worry. They got the computers, the faxes, the telex lines, everything. It was all tied in through the 324th. That's all she wrote. Our tooth-to-tail logistics are shot."

Around the room, the faces of Chiun, Sheik Fareem, and Prince Imperator Bazzaz looked as blank as three slices of Wonder Bread.

"We have no inventory control!" Hornworks snapped.

If anything, their blankness increased.

"We don't know where anything is!" Hornworks shouted in exasperation. "Or was. That means munitions, rations, armor, rolling stock, the whole shebang. Including our compaign plans. They were all on hard disk. I'm sick, I tell you. My pension just went south. We're reduced to war-gaming with an abacus, if we had one."

"Ah," said Chiun, the sheik, and the imperator general in unison. The Master of Sinanju turned to the sheik.

"Have you an abacus to lend this unfortunate white?" he asked.

The sheik nodded. "For a price."

The Master of Sinanju told Praetor Hornworks, "You shall have your abacus, praetor. Take heart. Your problem is solved."

"Wonderful," growled Hornworks. "That ain't all the bad news. Maddas Hinsein just appeared on the TV. He's alive and kicking. We're back to square one."

"No," said Chiun, lifting a wise finger, "for I have a brilliant plan!"

"And the dang Iraitis have a zillion Scuds all ready to go. They may be neolithic by our standards, but they'll kill us just as dead as neutron bombs."

"You have neutron booms?" asked Chiun, wispy beard atremble.

"Sure, can I use them? Assuming I can find them now."

"No!" said Chiun firmly. "Consign them all into the Gulf!"

"Then let me unleash our air assets," Hornworks pleaded. "Please. We gotta knock out those Scuds fast! We can do it inside of a day, maybe three. We have Wild Weasels, Ravens, Skyhawks, Blackhawks, Tomcats, Eagles, Flying Falcons, Cobras and Jaguars, all set to go."

"I will not risk the lives of innocent animals in a war not of their making," Chiun said flatly.

"But we can own the skies!"

"Let the enemy have the sky," proclaimed the Master of Sinanju in a triumphant voice. "We will take the ground."

"Yes," said Sheik Fareem sagely. "We want nothing of the sky." The old sheik turned to his adopted son. "Are you in agreement, my son?"

"Absolutely. There is no oil in the sky."

Praetor Hornworks blinked. His eyes narrowed craftily.

"How about Apaches?" he asked. "And maybe a few Tomahawks? At least let me use the tip of the spear."

"This is not a Wild West movie," Chiun sniffed. "I will not allow the noble but oppressed red man to be dragged into the white man's folly."

"I suppose warthogs are out of the question?"

"Did you hear that, Father?" exclaimed Prince Imperator Bazzaz. "The infidels have brought pigs onto Moslem sand."

"They're just called warthogs," Hornworks said hastily. "They're actually tank-killer planes. The A-10 Thunderbolt is the official designation. What is it about you guys and pigs, anyway?"

"Moslems are taught that the mere touch of swine is an abomination that will make us unclean and unprepared to enter Paradise," explained Bazzaz solemnly.

"How can it be called Paradise if you can't chow down on ham and eggs?" Praetor Hornworks wondered aloud.

The prince imperator and the sheik turned pale and looked away.

The Master of Sinanju interrupted. "No noisy machines that fly will be allowed in the legions I envision."

"How about a blimp or two?" Praetor Hornworks asked sarcastically. "Nice fat harmless blimps. Unarmed."

Chiun's hazel eyes narrowed.

"Yes," he said slowly. "There might be a place for blimps in my great plan. Yes. You have my permission to do this."

"Good. Maybe we can laugh the Scud crews into helplessness."

"Possibly," Chiun said vaguely. "Have you fulfilled my instructions?"

"Your what? Oh, yeah. The silent Scud killer. How could I forget those? I got a couple in my back pocket here, courtesy of the good ol' CIA."

Praetor Hornworks dug into his back pocket, extracting a pair of thick silver tubes, sealed at one end with black caps.

Prince Praetor Bazzaz accepted one of these from his American counterpart. He looked it over, as Chiun took the other, curiosity wrinkling his tiny visage.

The sheik watched as his adopted son removed the black cap, sniffed the exposed tip, and recoiled from the pungent smell.

"If you can get special operations personnel to those Scud launchers armed with one of these little doodads," said Hornworks confidently, "our problems could be solved in jig time."

"It is a Magic Marker, this doodad?" asked Bazzaz, for once encountering an odor stronger than his own.

"It may be a marker, but magic it isn't," said Praetor Hornworks flatly. "Officially, they're called LME's."

"Ah," said Prince Imperator Bazzaz. "I understand now. Poisoned food. We trick the enemy into eating these, and they are dead."

"You're thinking of MRE's—meals ready to eat. Obviously you tasted some."

Bazzaz made a face, saying, "I barely survived."

"Anybody who mistakes an LME for a Popsicle gets a bite of death," Hornworks said confidently. "How many will do you? I can get you as many of these as you want."

"As many as there are launchers for these Scum missiles," Chiun told him.

"Cruds. I mean Scuds." Hornworks threw up his hands. "I don't know what I mean. I think I'm having a nightmare."

"Nightmares come from eating pork chops," said Prince Imperator Bazzaz sanctimoniously.

Praetor Hornworks, who happened to enjoy pork chops, especially smothered in applesauce, was searching his mind for an unoffending comeback when an orderly ran into the room waving and shouting.

"The Iraitis are on the move!"

"What?"

"Sir, they're pouring over the Maddas Line like a million ants," said the orderly.

"They're advancing? These are dug-in defensive

troops! Why the hell are they advancing? They should be making us come to them!"

"Because they are led by an imbecile," said Sheik Fareem wisely. "Have you not come to understand this?"

"I'm still trying to get used to the SOB still being on the planet." He turned to the orderly. "Don't just stand there, decurion! Let's get some tactical computers in here!"

"Begging your pardon, Gen . . . I mean Praetor, but all the computers are off-line. We're blind as bats, tactically speaking."

Hornworks slapped his broad forehead in disgust. "My God! That's right! What the blazes are we going to do?"

"The answer is to be found in this very room," said the Master of Sinanju gravely.

Hornworks whirled. His eyes went to his imperator's long pointing finger. He followed an invisible line starting at the tip of the nail to a nearby table. There sat the tortoiseshell.

Eyes widening, Praetor Hornworks made a wild dash for it.

"The goldang shell!" he shouted. "It ain't much, but it's all the battle plan we got!"

Carefully he brought it back to where the others were seated. He set the shell in the center of the rug, orienting it so that it was aligned with true north.

There was an olive-drab tactical field phone at his elbow. He picked it up and began issuing orders, his eyes riveted to the cracked and dappled old shell that reminded him of a petrified leopard.

"Get me the Ninth Hispana Legion," he said firmly. "Indiana."

And where he sat, Chiun, Reigning Master of Sinanju, allowed himself a wan smile. The man was actually performing his task correctly. Who said whites were uneducable?

# 24

General Shagdoof Aboona was utterly confident of victory.

His uniform was British, purchased in bulk from the United Kingdom after a thoughtless vice chancellor decided to clear out one of her majesty's Royal Army warehouses, thus leaving the British forces with only woodland camos. His assault rifle was Soviet. Air cover would be provided by Soviet MiGs, as well as French Mirages. He possessed American Stinger ground-to-air missiles liberated from Kurani stockpiles. His war-gas stockpiles were German. Chinese silkworms guarded Irait's tiny coast.

It was remarkable, he thought.

The UN had had to form a thirty-nation anti-Irait coalition to assemble such impressive firepower. And still they lacked Russian equipment.

From his control bunker behind the line of earthworks, mine fields, tank trenches, and concertina wire spirals, General Aboona exuded confidence. Only weeks before, he had been a simple cobbler from Duurtbagh. When the criminal coalition forces had massed themselves on the new southern border of Irait, every able-bodied Iraiti had been conscripted into the Popular People's Popular Auxiliary. Since it was a brand-new element, it naturally needed generals. Because he was taller than most Iraitis,

Shagdoof Aboona went right to the top, acquiring three stars of silvered paper on his British epaulets.

"I am very proud," said General Aboona on the day his Precious Leader personally placed the stars on his epaulets. After licking the backs. "This could happen only in Irait."

When he had learned that he was to go to the front, General Aboona had experienced a twinge of misgiving. But the sight of the massive Maddas Line had been as fortifying to his spirits as it had been to the new border.

No power could breach it. And since the Popular People's Popular Auxiliary was strictly a defensive force, he felt safer here than in Irait, where one could be shot for odd reasons.

His feeling of complacency lasted less than two months. Then came the call from President Maddas Hinsein.

"I have orders for you, brave one," had said Maddas Hinsein.

"Allah be praised," said Aboona, saluting the telephone.

"You are destined to lead your nation into greatness."

"I am ready," said Aboona, holding his salute, lest the call was a test of his loyalty.

"At dawn you will lead the entire PPPA from your berms and bunkers and pour over the Hamidi border like the conquerors you are."

Aboona blinked. "But, Precious Leader, we have spent weeks building these fortifications. Is is not better to wait out the cruel sanctions?"

"It is better to be victorious," Maddas countered. "I have the exact deployment of the UN forces. They will not expect you. And the unexpected is our chief weapon in the great sheik of struggles to come."

General Shagdoof Aboona looked toward his Soviet Kalashnikov, thinking that he had been mistaken all along.

"I fear I am not worthy of this honor," he stammered.

"Do not fret, brother," came the unreassuring voice of Maddas Hinsein, "the Renaissance Guard is at all times at your back."

"Yes, of course they are," said Aboona, thinking that they were there, not to back him up, but to shoot him in the back if he did not advance. "It will be done as you command."

"Was there any doubt?" asked Maddas Hinsein, terminating the connection.

General Shagdoof Aboona replaced the receiver with the realization that he was cannon fodder, and had been all along. He went to the full-length mirror in his command bunker, noticing powdery sand on his fine British war-surplus uniform. He brushed himself off. All but one of the paper stars of silver fell to the floor. He could not understand why this kept happening, but he no longer cared.

He wished now for the first time that he was back in Duurtbagh, a simple cobbler again.

Then, tears in his eyes, he picked up his Soviet assault rifle and went to give the orders that would probably cause his own troops to contemplate fixing their sights on the small of his back.

No matter what he did, he wore an invisible target on his spine. This was how Maddas Hinsein ruled his people.

# 25

The Battle of the Maddas Line went down in history as one of the most violent land engagements since Verdun.

It was also the briefest.

The Popular People's Popular Auxiliary poured over the line, shouting *"Allah Akbar!"* in loud voices and firing wildly into the air, in the hope that the UN forces would retreat from their fierce din. It was their only chance, they knew. If they fired toward the enemy, the enemy would probably shoot back. There were rumors that this was sometimes done in wars.

Such was the vastness of the desert that their cries went immediately undetected.

What alerted the waiting forces was the sounds of the PPPA attackers setting off their own antipersonnel mines. The mines had been laid by the Renaissance Guard under cover of darkness so the PPPA could not safely defect. Many were ashamed of the occupation of peaceful Kuran.

Explosions lit up the sky. Distant reverberations carried south. Body parts flew in all directions. And the dreaded defensive mine fields of the Maddas Line were totally cleared—by unfortunate Iraitis.

Since there were more PPPA forces than there were antipersonnel mines, most of the Iraiti troops got through.

They lacked tanks, APC's and field artillery. And so they yelled.

General Aboona called instructions to his field commanders from the safety of his behind-the-line bunker. When his soldiers had proved too demoralized to back-shoot him, he decided not to press his luck.

"The First Armored Division is located to the south!" he exhorted. "Attack at will, brave ones. Captain Amzi, take your unit to Point Afar, where only a squad of marines lie dug in. You will overwhelm them manfully."

It was a good plan.

Except that where the division should have been was a force of less than brigade strength. And the squad of marines was a squad no longer. He did not know what it was. There were no forces of four hundred soldiers in either the American or Iraiti table of organization.

Discovering itself facing a mere brigade, the PPPA, emboldened, charged with bayonets fixed. The enemy pulled back. PPPA lungs shouting victory, they closed in for the kill.

And fell victim to the classic pincer maneuver first used by Hannibal during the Battle of Cannae to defeat the Roman Army. Two wings of the divisions rolled out of the night to encircle the PPPA in a ring of steel. The carnage was brief. The handful of survivors surrendered, which was an excellent decision inasmuch as they had few bullets and their bayonets kept falling off.

Meanwhile, in the face of the unexpectedly overmanned marine squad, Captain Amzi's PPPA unit was pounded into so much camel fodder by howitzer fire and mortar rockets. He died wondering what kind of unit it was he was fighting.

It was an *ala*, not that that would have meant anything to him.

After an hour of hearing the rattle of small-arms fire and the boom of 105-millimeter tank cannon coming through his walkie-talkie, General Shagdoof Aboona gave up issuing orders and began requesting battle damage assessments.

He could hear his brave fellow Iraitis clearly. Their shrill, uncomprehending cries could mean only one thing.

It was a slaughter.

General Shagdoof Aboona heard the ringing of the direct line from the Palace of Sorrows as if through deep water.

Sunken-eyed, he picked up his Kalashnikov, plunked himself down on the side of his bunk, and, with the insistent ringing faint in his ears, put the cold bitter muzzle into his mouth and fumbled for the trigger with a nerveless thumb.

The hollow-point lifted the top of his head like the lid off a crockery cookie jar.

He was the final casualty of the Battle of the Maddas Line—elapsed time: eighty-six minutes and twelve seconds.

# 26

Praetor Winfield Scott Hornworks burst into the war room of the UN central command base.

"It worked! The Ninth Hispana Legion ground them into sand stew. And the Vermont Victrix ambushed the rest. Changing the order of battle was the smartest thing we could've done!"

The Master of Sinanju looked up from the tortoiseshell that lay at his feet. Sheik Fareem and Prince Imperator Bazzaz had repaired to the safety of a bunker.

"Show me," Chiun directed, no joy on his face.

"Sure thing." Hornworks strode over to the rug and sat himself down happily. Using his finger, he indicated several points on the spotted shell. They were exactly where the opposing cracks crossed.

"We stopped them here, here, and there. Just like on this road-kill thing here." He looked on, cocking an eye at the old Korean, who had earned his respect as had no other military officer since his father, George Armstrong "Buster" Hornworks, had paddled his behind for smoking cornsilk. "How'd you work these tactics out in advance? Astrology?"

"No," said Chiun absently. "I simply heated the shell in a brazier until it cracked."

Hornworks batted his eyes. "You mean that's all?"

"Of course not," spat the Master of Sinanju. "I first

prayed to the gods for guidance. This form of divination has been the way of my people since before the sun source was revealed to Wang the Great."

"Well, however it works, it beats computers any day of the durn week." The praetor grinned expansively. "So what's next? Tea leaves? Palm reading? You say it and we'll do it."

Chiun shook his aged head, saying, "The enemy has been discouraged. But he is not beaten. I have been charting the stars and they tell me that a new personality is about to enter the lists."

"Yeah? Who? And if it's Gorbachev, we're in deep dogfood."

"I do not know this one's name. But her moon is in Aquarius."

"Is that bad?"

"For us, no. For our foes, possibly. For Taurus and Aquarius are in conflict, signifying delay and frustration."

"So we wait for his next move, is that it?" Hornworks grunted.

"No. We must move swiftly to stage the grand plan I have devised to win the day."

"This may not be the best time to bring this up, but there's an old general's saying: No battle plan ever survived contact with the enemy."

"And there is a saying in my village: No enemy ever survived contact with the House of Sinanju," Chiun retorted.

"Since your notion got us through the night, my faith's in you," Praetor Hornworks said quickly.

"Have the LEM's arrived?" Chiun asked.

"LME's. On their way. I scrounged up as many of 'em as I could. Just give the word, and I'll assign special teams to take 'em into the field. I suggest good old Army Rangers. Marines would probably lose every blamed one before they even got to the target sites."

The Master of Sinanju gathered his kimono skirts about his pipestem legs. "No. You will give them to me."

"All of them?"

"Exactly. Then you will arrange to convey me into beleaguered Kuran. I will pass out these devices to the forces I have selected."

"What forces? Beyond the neutral zone, there's nothing but unfriendlies."

"Yes. But the question is, who is unfriendly to whom?"

Praetor Hornworks took off his service cap and scratched his bristled skull.

"Listen, I can't let you go into Kuran. You're the best blasted field officer in this man's legion."

"I must. For my son is in that cruel land."

"Didn't you hear? All the hostages are out."

"Not all," Chiun said firmly. "And I am going. You are a soldier. Obey your imperator."

Praetor Hornworks struggled to his feet. He was getting too old for all this squatting and kneeling, but if it brought results, it was better than being up on the line.

"I'm on it," he said. He started for the phone, then turned, his eyebrows lifting quizzically.

"You say this new person is a gal?" he asked Chiun.

"So the stars foretell."

"What kind of gal could help out ol' Maddas?"

"The wrong kind."

"Good point. You know, even if this highfalutin plan of yours comes off, this fracas ain't gonna be over until someone up and nails that son of a camel."

Chiun's eyes glinted with a sudden cold light.

"Someone will," he said.

"We generals got another saying: In times of crisis, a leader's assassin is already at his side, but neither man knows it."

"The one who will dispatch the Mad Arab is not yet at his side," the Master of Sinanju intoned. "But soon, soon. . . ."

# 27

When the last Air Irait jet returned from the outside world, the pilot and copilot emerged from the cockpit to face a pair of scarlet-bereted Renaissance Guard troopers.

"You have been sentenced to death *in absentia*," announced the first guard. "The stated crime is releasing Western hostages without permission."

"Allah! But we were acting upon direct instructions of *al-Ze'em*," the pilot protested.

"*Al-Ze'em* is no more," the other trooper explained. "Our Precious Leader has resumed supremacy over proud Irait."

The two pilots turned green as they were marched out onto the deserted concourse, stood up before a ticket counter, and shot down in cold blood. There they turned white as the blood flowed from their bodies, replenishing the drying patch of rusty fluid left by their late colleagues.

An Air Irait maintenance worker later went about the task of cleaning up the bodies. He wondered who would fly the commercial airplanes now that virtually every civilian pilot had ended up in a common grave. He hoped it would be him. Although he could barely drive a car, it was possible. In Irait, where summary execution was the commonest instigator of career advancement, the Peter Principle had been raised to high art.

He was contemplating the next stage of his career as he was cleaning out the late pilot's aircraft.

From the women's room came a dull pounding and a high voice speaking excited English.

"Let me out!" it said. It was a woman's voice. He went to unlock the door.

Out stumbled, not a woman, but a slip of a girl wearing a black-and-white optical-print dress that made him think of old *Laugh-In* reruns.

"Who are you?" he asked in thick English.

"I'm Sky Bluel," said the girl in a breathless American accent. She wore her hair long and straight, a yellow ribbon holding it in place. Behind rose-tinted granny glasses her eyes were wide and innocent to the point of vacuousness.

"You are pink, not blue."

"Think of me as the Jane Fonda of the nineties," Sky Bluel added. "Now, quick, take me to your leader. I have a secret plan to end the war!"

"But . . . there is no war."

"That's my secret plan. It's outta sight!"

# 28

Kaitmast was an Afghani.

Kaitmast had been a simple goatherd when the brutal Russians had invaded his peaceful land. After his village was obliterated by a rocket attack, he joined the Hezb-i-Islami faction of the Afghan Mujahideen. Over the course of the 1980's Kaitmast had sent many a Russian soldier back to his motherland in the "Black Tulip"—the evacuation helicopter that bore the enemy dead from the field of battle.

With U.S.-supplied Stinger missiles, Kaitmast—whose name meant "Tough" in his native Afghani—had shot down a few Black Tulips too. Not to mention assorted MiGs.

Now the Russians had slunk back to their godless land, and the only foes left for Kaitmast to fight were the traitorous Afghan collaborators of the hated Soviet-backed regime.

Now that victory lay near, he felt almost sad. Kaitmast had grown quite fond of combat. He did not look forward to returning to the goats at all. Such was his mood after a decade of conflict.

It was a moonless night when Kaitmast heard the dull sounds rolling out of Pakistan.

He snapped out of his sleep, thinking that it was the rumble of T-72 tanks. A fighting grin came over his battle-hardened features. Perhaps it was the *Shouroui*—the Soviets—he thought, returning for more sport. Could their soldiers have grown bored with peace as well?

His Kalashnikov cradled across his crooked elbows, Kaitmast crawled along the high barren crags of the Khyber Pass. Reaching a point of vantage, he peered down into Pakistan, his squint eyes eager.

What he saw made him blink in wonderment.

But what he heard froze his blood.

It was a high eerie keening. The winds through the eternal Khyber might have produced such beauteous sounds. It filled the clear night air like a dark wine of song.

"Allah!" Kaitmast muttered, not immediately comprehending. And because he feared what he did not understand, he lifted his AK-47 and, setting it to fire single shots, began to snipe into the great dark shape that moved inexorably toward the Khyber Pass.

Strangely, there was no return fire, no faltering of the ground-shaking thunder or the unearthly song that was like an intoxicating wine.

Kaitmast emptied his clip without result. Inserting another, he emptied that too. But it was like shooting at the wind. He began to grow afraid.

The song and the thunder did not abandon the Khyber Pass until long after the sun had risen the next morning.

When it did, it illuminated the cold cadaver of Kaitmast, the Afghan freedom fighter. Or at least such pieces of Kaitmast as had landed where the sun's rays shone. Those ragtag Mujahideen who found him later that day thought to themselves that a human being could be rendered into such ruin only by being drawn and quartered by wild horses and then the separate pieces chewed by ravenous wolves.

And when they went to see what had done this to their brave comrade, they discovered spoor like a great winding serpent track that was dotted with ill-smelling lumps of excrement.

It led deep into the heart of Afghanistan.

Over hot tea flavored with sour yak butter, they conferred over how best to deal with this incursion. After long argument, the freedom fighters were split, and they went their separate ways, each group to act upon its best judgment.

Those who elected to follow it were never heard from again.

Those whose curiosity was less keen lived.

Neither forgot to the end of their days the song they were privileged to hear.

# 29

The decurion brought the Master of Sinanju a butyl rubber gasproof environment suit and matching gas mask.

Laying these before Chiun's feet, the decurion said, "Specially tailored to your size, sir. Since we're about the same height and build, I tried it on to be sure. It fits me."

The Master of Sinanju poked at the ugly slick material of the suit disapprovingly. He had seen its like before, months ago, in the doomed town in Missouri that had been decimated by deadly gases. It had been the start of the assignment that had brought him to a near-death in the cold water of a peaceless eternity.

Inwardly the Master of Sinanju shuddered at the thought. These last few months had been an ordeal. First the death that was not, and then the loss of Remo. He had seen the television transmission from cursed Abominadad, showing Remo and the girl who was Kali, their skins black in death. All was lost. All was over. One last mission and his work would be done. He would return to his humble village to live out the remaining days of his difficult life, childless and bitter.

Chiun looked up toward the decurion's expectant face.

"I do not intend to wear such an abomination," he said sternly. "I asked only to examine one of these monstrosities."

"But you have to, sir. The Apache's waiting to ferry you into Indian country. The Iraitis have gas up there."

"Then let them look to their diets," sniffed the Master of Sinanju.

"Sir?"

"Never mind," Chiun sighed. It had been a rare joke, to dispel his bitter mood. But the decurion did not find humor in it. That was the trouble with the young. They never laughed at an old man's humor. Remo would not have laughed either, but at least he would not have stood before him stiff of mien and without a glint of intelligence on his pale round-eyed face.

Chiun sighed anew. His hazel eyes glanced at the goggle-eyed lenses of the gas mask and its round snout.

"Have you many of these?" he asked the dull decurion.

"Every soldier in the theater has been issued one, sir."

"And these smelly plastic garments?"

"Standard issue."

"These brown spots—can they be removed?"

"I doubt it, sir. They are desert camouflage. We can get you a woodland version if you'd prefer, but I recommend desert coloration if you're going to go poking around in the sand."

"Only a white could fail to spy a man walking through the desert dressed for rolling in the dungheaps," Chiun sniffed.

"Whatever you say, sir."

"Can these be painted?" Chiun asked at last.

"We could try."

Chiun indicated the gas mask with a clear fingernail. "And these mask contrivances?"

"Possibly."

"Have them painted at once," Chiun ordered. "And tell my worthy Apache guide to wait. He may sharpen his tomahawk if time hangs heavy on his hands."

The decurion gathered up the uniform, asking, "What color would you prefer, sir?"

"Pink."

"Pink?"

"You do have pink paint?" Chiun inquired.

"We may have to special-order," the decurion admitted.

"Then do this. I would also like several sheets of pink paper and a pair of shears."

"Do you want the shears to be pink too?" asked the puzzled decurion.

"Of course not!" snapped the Master of Sinanju indignantly. "One cannot prosecute a war with pink shears. Now, be gone."

"Yes, sir. Right away, sir."

The decurion left the room wearing an expression of doubt and confusion. He took comfort in the fact that he was no longer a mere orderly, but a decurion. He didn't know what it meant, but it sounded great to the folks at home.

It took less than an hour, but the gasproof suit was returned to the Master of Sinanju, gleaming a fresh pink color.

Praetor Winfield Scott Hornworks personally laid these items at his feet. He placed the shears and pink construction paper atop the pink pile. The colors matched to within a shade.

"I heard you decided against going," Hornworks said. "Smart move. A man's gotta know his limitations, especially one your age."

"I have not," returned Chiun, picking up the shears. He began cutting the top sheet into a long pink triangle.

"How long you gonna wait, then? We got a lot of Scuds to kill, and ol' Maddas ain't exactly gonna wait for the Mahdi to return before he makes his move."

The Master of Sinanju cut a second sheet into an identical pink triangle.

"I have thought long on the way to defeat the foe we face," he said slowly.

"You ask me, this is a simple matter. Just go in and defang him."

Chiun frowned in concentration. "Maddas Hinsein has the sun in Taurus. If you cut off his hand, he will tell himself that he still possesses his remaining hand."

"So? We chop his legs out from under him."

"Then he will tell himself that as long as he has his brain, he is not defeated. Thus, you must lop off his head—which is what you should have done in the first place." Chiun cut a circle in the third sheet, and holding it up to Praetor Hornworks' uncertain gaze, punctured it with a pair of upraised fingers. Two identical ragged holes were created.

"That's what I been trying to get you to do all along," Hornworks said, throwing up his hands. "We gotta go after his command and control structure. Decapitate him from his army. It's a dang autocracy up there. Without Maddas, they'll fall apart."

Chiun studied his handiwork briefly and looked up. "You think we should cut off his head?"

"Not literally," Hornworks admitted. "It's not the American way to go after heads of state, personal-like."

"Then you do not know how to wage these kinds of wars," Chiun snapped.

The Master of Sinanju picked up the gas mask and the cut pieces of paper.

"If I command it," he said slowly, "could all these garments be made into this color?"

"Sure. But why would we want to? I'm anticipating a desert campaign, not a ladies' social."

"Because these garments are essential to the liberation of Kuran."

"They are?"

"According to my plan, no shots need be fired, no blood spilled."

"I like your thinking, even if I can't hardly follow it. But taking Kuran without firing a blamed shot—it would be easier to teach a pig to whistle 'Dixie.' And you know what they say about that."

Arching one faint eyebrow, the Master of Sinanju looked up as he affixed the pink triangles to the temples of the mask so they hung point-down.

"No? What do they say?"

"It won't work and you'll annoy the pig." Praetor Hornworks cracked a lopsided grin that was not returned.

The Master of Sinanju slapped the perforated circle over the silver canister of the mask intake. It stayed in place, held only by the adhesive power of his saliva.

"That is an excellent idea," he said absently.

"What is?"

"Teaching pigs to whistle. It is a brilliant stroke."

"Not that I ever noticed. And I'm from Tennessee."

"While I am away," said the Master of Sinanju, coming to his feet like pale incense wafting ceilingward, "it will be your assigned task to teach the pigs to whistle."

"What pigs?"

"The Pigs of Peace, of course."

"You ain't by chance got yourself confused with the dogs of war, now have you?"

"Certainly not. And if you can command Wild Weasels and other such beasts, why not Peace Pigs?"

Although Praetor Hornworks did not exactly follow the old Korean's logic, neither could he defeat it.

And so he asked, "Any particular tune, sir?"

"You may select one of your own choosing," Chiun said dismissively. "I will agree to delegate that task to you, since the liberation of Kuran is not dependent upon the song the pigs whistle, only that they whistle."

"I've always been partial to 'Bridge over the River Kwai,' myself."

"Acceptable. Now please summon the decurion."

"You're leaving?"

"Soon. But I wish him to try on this garment. It is a test."

"It's sure something," said Hornworks, reaching for the phone.

The decurion struggled into the garment under the doubtful eye of Praetor Hornworks and the critical gaze of the Master of Sinanju.

When it was on, he asked, his voice muffled, "How do I look?"

"Ridiculous," said Hornworks in an unenthusiastic voice.

"Perfect," said the Master of Sinanju, beaming at his handiwork.

Hornworks put his hands on his hips and bellowed, "He looks like he's going to a durn pajama party with those pink flaps hanging down. And that circle is restricting his air flow. He needs more than two holes to breathe through."

The Master of Sinanju walked around the decurion several times in silent contemplation.

"It is missing something," he mused.

"What?" asked Hornworks acidly. "A propeller beanie?"

The Master of Sinanju went to a desk drawer and removed a pipe cleaner, which he twisted into a corkscrew shape. Returning to the decurion, he affixed it to the pink seat of the suit.

"Now you done it," Hornworks complained. "You just punctured that man's protection. The suit's integrity is shot now."

"This is how you shall outfit your legions for the taking of the enemy *limes.*"

Praetor Hornworks wrinkled his sweat-smeared brow. "*Limes?*" He searched his memory. "Oh, yeah, the frontline troops. My Latin is still rusty. We gonna laugh the enemy into submission, are we?"

"You are obviously an unimaginative lout. Summon the sheik and his son."

"Sure. Just let me put on my own gas mask. That dang Ay-rab has taken to bathing in Aqua Velva lately."

A moment later, Sheik Fareem and Prince Imperator Bazzaz started through the doorway.

On the threshold they came to a dead stop, their gaze drawn automatically to the ludicrous pink figure of the decurion. Their sloe orbs flew wide.

"Allah!" the sheik cried, clutching his brown-and-red robes.

"Blasphemy!" echoed Bazzaz. *"Khazir!"*

Faces filled with fright, they backed away. The door slammed. Their frantic feet could be heard receding the full length of the corridor.

The Master of Sinanju turned to Praetor Hornworks, asking, "Do you understand now?"

Praetor Hornworks' chin did not quite touch the rug, but it hung slacker than a discarded marionette's jaw. With equal woodenness he pivoted toward the startled decurion.

"Son, think you can whistle the 'Bridge over the River Kwai'? Let's hear a few bars for your kindly praetor."

An hour later, the Master of Sinanju strode toward a waiting Apache helicopter gunship.

"There's your Apache," Praetor Hornworks informed him.

"He looks like a Nubian," Chiun said, noting that the pilot was black.

"The LME's are all aboard. The pilot has orders to stick with you until the job's done and get you back in one piece."

"We will return separately. For I will continue on to Abominadad alone."

The Apache's rotors began whining in a gathering circle. Sand kicked up.

"What's up there?" Hornworks wanted to know.

"The man you wish me to decapitate."

"How you gonna do that without calling in the B-52's?"

"By calling another number entirely," said the Master of Sinanju, stepping into the rising rotor wash as if into a desert sandstorm. "Which I have done."

# 30

In the sleepy village of Sinanju, poised over the cold waters of the West Korea Bay, an unfamiliar sound arrived with the morning sun.

It brought the villagers from their fishing shacks and mud huts. Dogs barked. Children raced to and fro, as if to discover the source of the insistent bell under a rock or buried in the eternal mud that even the bitter cold of winter never completely hardened.

One man emerged from his hut with sleepy determination, however.

Stooped old Pullyang, caretaker of the village of Sinanju, Pearl of the East, Center of the Known Universe, trudged up the steep hill to the House of the Masters, which perched like a gem carved of rare woods on the low hillock that dominated the otherwise ramshackle village.

He muttered imprecations under his breath as he knelt before the ornate teak door, touching two panels with his forefinger. A concealed lock clicked. He removed a panel that revealed a long dowel of wood.

Only after old Pullyang had removed this obstructing dowel could the door be opened safely.

He passed into the close, musty atmosphere, where the insistent ringing continued more loudly.

A tall black object reposed on a low taboret. Pullyang

knelt before it in wonder. The rings continued, spaced apart, but untiring. He saw that the source of this ringing was like a candlestick with an ugly black flower sprouting at the top. The object was of a dull black material, like ebony.

Old Pullyang searched his mind for the proper ritual.

"Ah," he murmured, remembering. Speak to the flower and listen to the pestle.

He took up the candlestick, plucking the pestlelike object from the forked prong from which it hung. He clasped this to his ear and lifted the ugly unscented flower of a thing to his mouth, as he had been instructed so long ago.

The bothersome ringing instantly ceased.

Pullyang spoke. "Yes, O Master?"

A voice buzzed from the pestle. Pullyang listened.

"But . . ." he began. "I did not hear that you were dead. Yes, I know that you are not sojourning with your ancestors. I—"

Wincing, he flinched from the sharp quacking voice emanating from the ear device.

"Immediately, O Master Chiun," he said.

He replaced the device and went in search of a specific item in the dim room.

Around him stood the treasures of the ages. Fine silks. Gold in all manner of shape and form. Jewels in jars, in heaps, spilling from silken sacks, lay in profusion. Coins bearing the likenesses of emperors of renown and obscurity were stacked in an open chest, segregated into two piles—those who paid on time and those who did not.

The object of the old Korean's search hung in a place of honor.

It was a sword. Over seven feet long, with a thin blade that flared into a broad spade-shaped point.

The hilt was encrusted with exquisite emeralds and rubies.

Taking care not injure himself, old Pullyang took the

long ornate sword down from its silver pegs. Gingerly he bore it to a long ebony box and placed it within.

The interior of the box was molded to accept the sword. He clapped the lid shut and threw two brass hooks into eyelets, securing but not locking the box.

Then, after heating a bowl of wax, Pullyang affixed a seal atop the box. It was a simple device, a trapezoid bisected by a slash mark.

It was, he knew, better than the securest lock, more valuable that the most expensive stamp, and more fearsome than any written warning against theft.

It was the seal of the House of Sinanju and it would ensure that the sword reached its destination.

With a sharp stick dipped in the hot sticky wax, Pullyang inscribed the destination on top of the box:

TO PRESIDENT MADDAS HINSEIN
PALACE OF SORROWS
ABOMINADAD, IRAIT

Then he went in search of a messenger who would go to the outside world and summon a lackey of the North Korean government to start the sword on its way.

# 31

Saluda Jomart belonged to the Pesh Mergas. In Kurdish this meant: "Those Who Face Death."

For hundreds of years the Kurds had suffered at the hands of the Arabs and Turks. For a century they dreamed of establishing a new Kurdistan in the north of Irait. For thirty years they had been at war with Irait.

The cruel decrees of Maddas Hinsein were only the latest oppressor, but as oppressors went, Maddas was especially wicked. Not content to exterminate the Kurds through bloodshed and cruelty, he had unleashed his death gases upon simple Kurdish villages.

Saluda had nearly died from such terror when the Iraitis had attacked his home village in the Behinda Valley.

In those days, he had been the commander of an entire *surlek*—a company of one thousand men. After the gas had been blown away, leaving only black-skinned corpses, he was able to muster but a *lek* of 350 Kurds.

Now, after the conquest of Kuran, he was down to a mere *pal.* But fifty men. The others had been forcibly conscripted into the Iraiti Army. It was a final cruelty—to be forced to fight for the oppressor.

Still, Saluda looked forward to the day when these very Kurds would become vipers in the bosom of the oppressor who dared proclaim himself as modern Saladin—knowing that Saladin had been, not an Arab, but the mightiest of all Kurds.

Saluda crouched in the crags of a mountain, cradling his 7.98 mm. Brno rifle—which he had pried from his valiant father's dead hands after a firefight—when the sound of a helicopter assaulted his ears.

It did not sound like one of the oppressor's craft, so Saluda held his fire after he had crawled up to a place of advantage.

It was a small craft, flying low, looking like a great dark shark of the sky. The markings were not Iraiti.

It settled in the sand, throwing up sandy billows, not far from a village on the banks of the Shin River.

Saluda clambered down from the mountain. Too late. The dark shark had already lifted off.

But it had left behind a man and many boxes.

Approaching cautiously, Saluda the Kurd saw that the passenger was an old man with strange narrow eyes. He stood resolute, chin up, his venerable white hair waving in the hot wind. He wore white, a color of bad omen.

"I see by the pattern of your turban that you are a Kurd of the Barzani tribe," the little man said calmly, oblivious of the deadly maw of the Brno.

"Spoken truly," said Saluda, whose red-and-white-checkered turban marked him as a warrior who never ran from battle. "And who might you be, strange man with strange eyes who speaks the tongue of my people?"

"I am Chiun. My ancestors knew yours when they waxed mighty and were called the Medes."

"Those days are all but forgotten, *mamusta*," Saluda said, respect softening his voice.

The stranger cocked his head curiously. "Is the House of Sinanju, too, forgotten?"

"Not forgotten, but the memory dims."

"Then let it shine anew from this day forward," said the Master of Sinanju, gesturing broadly to the wooden crates that lay in the dust. "For in these simple boxes I have brought liberation for your people and doom for the tyrant Maddas. Enough weapons for several *surleks.*"

"Alas," said Saluda, lowering his weapon, "I command but a *pal* these evil days."

"You have friends? Other commanders?"

"Many. Even ones in the hated Iraiti Army."

"This is better than I hoped, for these weapons are of use only against the dreaded Crud missiles of the scum oppressor."

With a curved knife, Suluda broke open one crate. He squinted at rows of the silver-and-black tubes within.

"What will these do?" he wondered aloud, taking one in hand.

"They will break the back of the evil one," promised Chiun. "And even a child may wield them to good use."

Insulted, Saluda spat, "Then seek you children for your tricks. The men of Kurdistan are warriors."

"No offense was intended, O Kurd. Your warriors need only use these to write their names in the pages of history."

Saluda removed the cap. The smell offended his nose. He went over to a rock and inscribed his name. The tip left a moist colorless trail that quickly faded to nothingness.

"This must be a mighty instrument for writing if it leaves no mark on stone, but inscribes one's name on the pages of history," Saluda muttered.

"If you are not man enough to wield it," Chiun retorted, "I will find another."

"Man enough?" Saluda flared. "I will scour the caves and foothills and find you *surleks* of men who are not afraid of making history!"

The Master of Sinanju drew himself up with quiet dignity. "Spoken like a true son of the Medes," he intoned. "I have found the Kurd who will cause the Wheel of Destiny to complete a full revolution."

# 32

Naseem wore his Iraiti uniform like a hair shirt.

Hauled away from his village by the Iraiti conscriptors, he was given an ill-fitting uniform in exchange for his fine fringed turban and baggy woolen costume, and an old Enfield rifle with no bullets.

With this insult of a weapon, he was set to guarding a sand-painted bunker where a great rolling Scud missile launcher was held in readiness.

But in his back pocket he had a silver tube given to him by a fellow Kurd named Mustafa. His instructions were as simple as they were inexplicable.

When night fell, Naseem steeled himself to enter the bunker. He was not afraid, for since he was a boy he had heard the Kurdish proverb "The male is born to be slaughtered." If he was killed, this was to be.

The bunker door was not locked, for easy egress of the launcher on short notice. Naseem simply entered.

Setting his useless rifle by the door, he slipped up to the launcher and climbed atop the great buff-colored missile which lay flat on its movable rail.

Lying on his stomach, he uncapped the silver tube and began writing out his name. He wrote large, according to his instructions. He had been told that he would be writing his name in history, and because the world had long ago forgotten the Kurds, rightly called "the orphans of the universe," he wrote very, very big.

For he knew that all over Irait and Kuran, his Kurdish brothers were doing the very same thing to other Scuds and Iraiti strike aircraft.

# 33

President Maddas Hinsein slammed down the field telephone receiver after the 1,785th unanswered ring.

"That traitor Aboona refuses to answer!" he roared.

All around the council room, his high command jumped in their seats. This included Vice-President Juniper Jackman and Information Minister Don Cooder, who were experiencing what Maddas had referred to as "orientation."

Maddas turned to his new information minister, who wore a Maddas Hinsein mustache that had been applied with black shoe polish.

"Explain this!" he demanded in Arabic.

"What's he saying?" Cooder asked Jackman nervously.

"No clue. I'd just start talking, was I you," Jackman said.

"Well, you see, your grace," Don Cooder began, "as I see it—and we must be careful with our facts here, because events are unfolding too rapidly to assimilate them in coherent sequence . . ."

The foreign minister translated on the fly.

Maddas received the rambling account with a grim face. Since it did not contradict him, he took no exception. He was used to his ministers talking much but saying little. That is why he always had the council-room

TV tuned to CNN—it was his only source of reliable intelligence.

He pulled the remote from a belt holster, causing most of the room to duck instinctively. The CNN logo came on. The council clambered back into their seats, features dripping cold perspiration.

They all watched in silence as the foreign minister essayed a running translation while patting his face with a handkerchief.

"We are thwarted," said Maddas Hinsein, after hearing of the failure to take Hamidi Arabia.

"A temporary setback," the foreign minister said quickly.

"Which you will surely overcome, Precious Leader," added the defense minister.

Maddas nodded.

"We must devise a new strategy to confound the infidel," he went on unhappily.

"Your brilliance will prove superior to their base perfidy," said the agriculture minister. "As always."

Vice-President Jackman leaned over to Don Cooder. "I can't tell what these mutton-munchers are saying, can you?"

"Shhh!" Cooder hissed. "You want to get us shot?"

"They won't shoot me. I'm vice-president now. I'm indespensable."

"Tell it to Dan Quayle."

That thought gave Iraiti Vice-President Jackman pause.

"I'm also a personal friend of Louis Farakhan," he pointed out. "That's as good as a free pass in this neck of the desert."

The voice of Maddas Hinsein intruded on their whispering.

"We must make a glorious gesture," he announced. "The eyes of the Arab world are on us now. How can we smash the aggressor? Come, come, I must have suggestions."

"We could send the Renaissance Guard south," the health minister offered, carefully. "If you think we should."

"Good. And then what?"

"They must take up the defense of the Maddas Line and our new thirteenth province before the hated aggressor overruns our position."

"A waste of good soldiers. Have more PPPA conscripts sent to the front. They are like the dinars in my pocket. Of use only when they are being spent. Our best must remain in readiness for the great sheik of struggles to come."

"We could blow up the oil wells in Kuran," the defense minister suggested.

"What good would that do?" asked Maddas Hinsein.

"It would make a wonderful series of explosions. Perhaps if there was no oil in Kuran, the Americans would have no reason to stay and vex us so."

Maddas Hinsein considered this novel thought at length.

The man who had ventured the suggestion had put it forth only because he had been put on the spot. He knew that such a deed would infuriate the world. But in a choice between infuriating the world and annoying his Precious Leader, it was no contest. The world was not sitting across the table from him.

"I will consider this," said Maddas Hinsein. "It is a good idea."

A servile knock on the door interrupted the next speaker.

"Come," said Maddas Hinsein.

A red-bereted Renaissance Guardsman entered. "Precious Leader, we have found an American girl on one of the returning planes. She desires to speak with you."

"Good. Have her tortured. I will speak with her afterward."

"At once, Precious Leader. But she has said that she has a plan to end the war."

Hearing this, Maddas Hinsein broke out into a bristly smile. He laughed. The laugh grew into a roar, which traveled around the room like insane wildfire.

"She wishes to end the war and there is no war!" Maddas roared. "She does not understand the proud Iraiti people. We want war! We revel in war. We look forward to war."

"Yes, we revel in war," chorused the Revolting Command Council, which believed no such thing.

"She says she is an expert in things nuclear," the guardsman added.

Maddas Hinsein swallowed his laughter. There were only two words that riveted his attention. The word "nuclear" happened to be one of them. "Torture" was the other.

"Bring her," he said quickly, his face returning to its natural sober cast.

The girl was brought in. Her stark optical-print dress made their vision swim, as if they stared at her through a disturbed pond. The yellow ribbon in her hair made Maddas Hinsein frown darkly.

"Hi, I'm Sky Bluel," she said brightly. "Peace."

"Uh-oh," said Don Cooder, recognizing the girl.

The foreign minister stood up. In thick English he asked, "You are a U.S. scientist?" His tone was skeptical.

"Actually I'm a student at USC," Sky admitted. "But I did grad work at Lawrence Livermore Laboratories—before I got booted out for kinda borrowing nuclear-weapons technology."

"You seem a mere girl."

"Physics majors can be girls—I mean, women—too." Sky looked past the foreign minister suddenly. "Hey, I know you! You're that over-thirty TV anchorpig. You helped me build a neutron bomb that got me into all that trouble. Tell them."

All eyes turned to Don Cooder.

"It's true," he said carefully. "I know this gal. She stiffed me. I helped her build a neutron bomb for demonstration purposes and she left town before airtime. We had to show a repeat." He made it sound like a leg amputation.

Maddas Hinsein interjected himself into this exchange with a gruff question. The foreign minister leaned over to explain the exchange.

While they huddled, Sky Bluel folded her arms. "For your information," she whispered to Don Cooder, "I was kidnapped. A lot of bad things happened. Palm Springs was almost wiped out. Someone died. And worst of all, I had to leave the country. My parents packed me off to Paris to study."

"My heart bleeds," said Don Cooder acidly.

Presently the foreign minister lifted his iron-gray head out of the huddle.

"You can build a neutron bomb?" he asked.

"If you got some tritium lying around, some beryllium oxide for the tamper, plastique. Oh, yeah, and steel for a combat casing."

"We do. But why would you do this for Irait? You are an American."

"That's the groovy part," Sky said excitedly. "The U.S. has nukes all around you, right?"

"This is true."

"So I build you a few neutron bombs, and presto—instant balance of power. They can't nuke you and you can't nuke them."

This kernel of invincible logic was passed on to Maddas Hinsein. His moist brown eyes went to the girl's innocent face. A crafty smile came over his fleshy caramel visage. He whispered in the foreign minister's ear.

The foreign minister bestowed his most disarming smile on Sky Bluel.

"Our Precious Leader," he said smoothly, "he sees the wisdom of your point of view. He wishes to know how soon you can build these peace-ensuring devices for us."

"Oh, a week," said Sky. "Maybe a month. Depends on what I have to work with."

"I thought you were antinuclear," Don Cooder whispered.

"I am. But I'm more antiwar. Listen: No blood for oil! USA out of Hamidi Arabia!" She lowered her voice. "Do I sound like Jane Fonda, or what?"

"You sound 'or what,' " Don Cooder snapped. "Definitely."

When Sky Bluel's words were translated, Maddas Hinsein's grin broadened. He clapped his hands loudly. He spoke at great length.

The foreign minister spoke next.

"Our Precious Leader has decided to put this to a vote in true democratic fashion. All in favor of delaying further military action in favor of building neutron bombs, say yes."

"I'm voting no," said Vice-President Jackman.

"Me too," Don Cooder chimed in. "This is ridiculous."

"All opposed will be issued service pistols along with one bullet."

"Why only one?" asked Cooder.

"Because when one wishes to commit suicide by pistol," he was told, "one bullet is all that is necessary."

"I vote yes," Cooder said instantly.

Vice-President Jackman raised an eager hand. "Make that two yeses."

In point of fact, it was unanimous.

This impressed Sky Bluel. "Wow! Ho Chi Minh's got nothing on you!"

As the foreign minister led Sky Bluel from the room, she asked a question in an uncertain voice.

"That stuff about suicide. That was a joke, right?"

"In Abominadad, we are always cutting up. I myself often thank Allah for providing us with a sense of humor second to none in the Arab world."

And the foreign minister smiled like a piranha eyeing legs in the water.

# 34

A day passed. Two. Three. A week. Two weeks.

As the world held its breath, America's industrial might geared up for the military mission destined to go down in the pages of history as Operation Dynamic Eviction.

An Ogden, Utah, factory went to around-the-clock shifts, turning out flamingo-pink butyl rubber gasproof suits outfitted with what appeared to be corkscrew antennas in the seat area. No one knew why.

In plants scattered throughout Iowa, Michigan, and elsewhere in America's heartland, specially customized pink gas masks rolled off assembly lines, were packed under the watchful eyes of armed MP's, and then loaded aboard C-5 Galaxy transports for the five-thousand-mile flight to Hamidi Arabia.

Idle Detroit auto factories received rush orders for unique fiberglass shells that were too big for ordinary stock cars and aerodynamically unsuited for small airplanes—the plant manager's second guess.

In Akron, Ohio, rubber capital of the world, customized blimps were rushed through the manufacturing stage and shipped flat, ostensibly for use in the next Rose Bowl parade. Their actual destination was the Star in the Center of the Flower of the Desert Military Base in Hamidi

Arabia, where they were inflated in the security of desert-camouflage bunkers.

The entire operation was mounted under the strictest security since the bombing of Tripoli. There were no leaks. This pleased the sector of official Washington that was privy to the plan.

Which did not include the Joint Chiefs of Staff in the Pentagon. They didn't have a clue. For the first time in the history of the United States, America was going to war and its high command was out of the loop.

But not completely out of the picture.

The chairman of the Joint Chiefs barged into the Tank, a green trash bag clutched in one fist.

"I got one!" he crowed. The Joint Chiefs gathered around a table as he emptied the contents into a table. They picked through it eagerly.

"It's pink!" mumbled the commandant of the Marines. "I can't have my men wearing one of these! The Navy will never let me live it down."

"What're these triangles hanging down?" asked the Army Chief of Staff, fingering one.

The Air Force Chief of Staff snapped his fingers. "Gotta be a gas-detection patch. Probably turns green at the first sign of chlorine."

"And this flexible squiggle in back must be some newfangled gas sensor," put in the chief of naval operations.

Everyone agreed that this had to be so.

But the pink coloration continued to baffle them. Outside of a guerrilla war in Miami Beach, no one knew of a combat environment in which flamingo pink was dominant.

But even more troublesome was the fact that the White House was keeping them in the dark about the operation to come.

At the White House, the President of the United States was out to callers—especially those emanating from the Pentagon.

He was on the cherry-red line to Folcroft Sanitarium and Harold Smith.

"So far, so good," he was saying. "General Hornworks says his troops will only need another day's training before they move north."

"Has there been any word of the Master of Sinanju since he went into Irait?" Smith asked.

"None. But I share your concern. It was a brave thing that he did, darn brave."

"Normally I would not be concerned, Mr. President. But after his lengthy ordeal, he is not up to par. When this is over, I fear he will be of little use to us in the field."

The President sighed. "Let's get through this crisis before we start fretting about the future. My biggest worry after this is over and done with is having our armed forces restored to normal. You should see the new table of organization. Reading it takes me back—to Mrs. Populious' ancient-history class."

"Of course, sir."

"Has there been any activity from Irait?"

"Nothing. A few broadcasts. They're continuing the pretense that Reverend Jackman and that anchor, Cooder, are now full-fledged members of the Revolting Command Council, but that's obviously a ploy to duck the hostage issue. But no military activity has been reported since the attempted border incursion. Let us hope it remains that way until Dynamic Eviction has been successfully concluded," Smith concluded tightly.

"You know, Smith, as crazy as this thing is, I can't help but feel absolute confidence in it," the President confided.

"The Master of Sinanju has never failed us yet."

The call was terminated. The world went back to counting the days and wondering what would happen next.

But apparently nothing happened. Not on the ground or in the air.

Only in space was a hint of future events picked up. Five hundred miles above the earth, an orbiting Lacrosse spy satellite detected an unusual plume of methane gas emanating from the interior of Afghanistan. It was tracking westward, but CIA analysts could not identify it. It seemed to be a natural phenomenon, but on a scale they had never before seen.

Because it was moving against the prevailing winds, a volcanic or lake-bed eruption was discounted. The only other possibility might have been droppings of a mighty herd of water buffalo. But a water-buffalo stampede of this magnitude had never been noticed before. There was no animal on earth large enough to panic that many cattle.

Throughout occupied Kuran and Irait, Kurdish warriors stole into aircraft revetments and Scud bunkers, writing their names invisibly and leaving the scenes of their depredations undetected by man or satellite.

And in Abominadad, Irait, a wooden crate arrived, addressed to President Maddas Hinsein.

# 35

President Maddas Hinsein was no fool.

When the wooden crate postmarked Pyongyang, North Korea, was delivered to the Palace of Sorrows, he had his most valuable council members open it while he descended to the German-made bunker under the palace, nicknamed the Mother of All Bunkers. He always selected his best men for this duty, because he knew it would deter them from shipping him bombs themselves.

Today his favorites happened to be the foreign minister and Vice-President Juniper Jackman.

Jackman was only too happy to take a crowbar to the crate. The line of AK-47's pointed in his direction constituted tremendous motivation.

"Bet Dan Quayle doesn't pull this kind of duty," he complained, confident he would not be shot because no one in the room understood English.

The planks split with a crack and revealed a magnificent sword as long as Kareem Abdul-Jabbar and encrusted with precious stones.

Maddas Hinsein was called up only after the sword had been safely removed, examined for venomous barbs, and dipped in a solution that would change color if a contact poison had been applied to the blade.

"It is a gift, Precious Leader," the foreign minister reported. "Truly. See?"

"The North Koreans obviously stand in solidarity with us," said the president of Irait with quiet satisfaction.

"Yet they claim otherwise. I have spoken with their ambassador and he knows nothing of this magnificent gift."

Maddas Hinsein frowned. "I will accept it anyway. Hang it over my desk in a place of honor."

"At once, Precious Leader."

When the sword was firmly in place, President Maddas Hinsein locked the door behind him and stood looking at the sword. He grinned. It was a worthy blade, and it gave him solace after the destruction of the crossed scimitars that had lifted so triumphantly over Arab Renaissance Square.

The sadness of that setback reminded the Scimitar of the Arabs of the treason of the four-armed Kimberly Baynes, and made him wistful for the corrective discipline of her quick, firm hands. With her gone, there was no one to spank him anymore.

Impulsively he went to a phone.

"The spider-armed girl," he demanded of his chief torturer, the minister of culture, "is her body still in the dungeon?"

"With the American assassin, as you commanded, Precious Leader."

"Do they . . . smell?"

"Strangely, no."

A quick smile broke over the president's dark face. "No? Hmmm. Perhaps I will torture them, then."

"Can one torture the dead?" wondered the culture minister, a hint of interest in his voice.

"If one has the stomach for it." Maddas Hinsein laughed, hanging up.

Down in the coolest part of the dungeon, the bodies lay on cold slabs of black basalt. Their skins were a remarkable flat black, as if powdered with coal dust.

The woman was completely nude. Maddas Hinsein dismissed the thought of mounting her. He had raped a cold corpse once, when he was a carefree young man. Never again, he vowed. He had caught a terrible cold.

The man lay composed in death, eyes closed, an austere look on his face. His colorful harem silks were in tatters, but Maddas Hinsein had no eyes for those. He noticed the large egglike bump in the center of his forehead. Obviously a bruise.

It was quite unusual, and the President of Irait could not resist poking it with his finger.

To his horror, it slid apart like a ruptured plum.

"Allah!" gasped the Scimitar of the Arabs, recoiling. For the bump had opened like a dead eyelid, revealing a sightless black orb. There had been no such organ on the man's brow in life, he recalled clearly.

As Maddas Hinsein backed away, black arms stirred like an upended lobster on the slab behind him. A naked chest shuddered, impelled by an indrawn breath.

The figure on the slab levered itself to a sitting position in silence, and blood-red eyes fell upon his unsuspecting back with a fiery regard.

*"You live . . ."* a dead voice whispered too low to be heard.

And a loud, frantic voice came from the corridor, crying, "O Scimitar of the Arabs! The impregnable Maddas Line is under attack!"

President Maddas Hinsein bolted from the torture room a mere flick ahead of grasping black nails.

# 36

If there was somone he could complain to without being shot for questioning authority, Colonel Hahmad Barsoomian of the Renaissance Guard would have complained loudly and vociferously.

But he figured he was in enough trouble as it was. His orders to report to the Maddas Line and take command of the ragtag Popular People's Popular Auxiliary could only mean he was regarded with suspicion by the high command. Why else would they exile him to work among undisciplined shopkeepers and teachers in ill-fitting uniforms?

It was night, and Colonel Barsoomian stood atop an earthen-mound breastworks scanning the neutral zone with his Zeiss military field glasses.

There was a crescent moon hanging low in the sky. It augured well, he thought. What little light it shed was like a shimmering silver rain collecting in the desert wadis below.

There was no sign of the anti-Irait UN forces. They would never attack. They feared to, Barsoomian was certain.

A low shape appeared in the sky. A glimmer of moonlight revealed it.

Colonel Barsoomian adjusted his glasses. It was silent

and oblate as a strayed moon. And it was coming this way.

"Searchlight crew!" he called down. "Direct your beam that way, you donkeys!"

A powerful tungsten light sprang to life. The beam wheeled southward, sweeping the sky.

"Left. Now right! There! Hold it there!" Barsoomian ordered.

And when the hot beam transfixed the floating silent thing, Colonel Barsoomian trained his binoculars upon it.

His jaw fell slowly at the terrible sight. His eyes grew round as coins. He could feel his heart pumping high in his throat.

"Shoot that blasphemous thing!" he commanded in a high, hoarse voice. "Bring it down!"

Orange-red tracers streaked through the night. And missed.

"Correct your aim, offspring of donkeys!"

The PPPA antiaircraft battery did. This time they fired wide in another direction, missing spectacularly.

Soon the thing was passing directly overhead and Barsoomian, seeing the four pink hooves looming directly over him, countermanded his order.

"Do not shoot! We do not want the unclean thing falling upon us!"

The order was unnecessary. The gunners were good Moslems. And they heard the continuous amplified squealing that the floating pink monster seemed to be making. It chilled the blood of every man along the long Maddas Line—for at strategic spots over the fortification, other silent pink monsters hovered like the most evil of omens.

Moslem faces turned skyward. Moslem mouths gaped in awe and fear. All eyes were on the silent monsters above.

And as if connected to a timer, the monsters all went *pop*! at once.

Shards of slick pink fleshlike matter began to fall. Soldiers scrambled for their holes, their bunkers. A few retreated from the line. Some ran screaming. No one stopped them. No one cared.

And when the commotion began to abate, the remaining defenders heard another sound.

It welled up from the south, out in the frontier. It was a kind of whistling, but great in its fullness and magnificence.

Colonel Barsoomian, thankfully untouched by the unclean pink rain, crawled up to the breastworks mound and employed his field glasses once more.

This time his mouth went round. For he saw the advancing host.

They were coming in a long skirmish line, thirty deep. It was a line that stretched in both directions, a wall of pink.

Pink legs marched in unison. Pink hands held M-16 assault rifles across pink chests. The rifles were not pink, but the faces above them were—pink, inflexible, and terrible. Eyes goggled glassily over pink snouts that were punctured by two pink-rimmed nostrils. Pink triangular ears flapped and beat against chubby pink cheeks as the pink soldiers advanced in an unbroken pink line.

And ahead of them, here and there, rumbled round pink monsters with identical beastlike snouted faces. They left trails in the sand like those of tracked vehicles. And they squealed and grunted and gave vent to "oink-oink" sounds that made Colonel Barsoomian's devout Moslem skin crawl as if from inquisitive ants.

But most terrible of all was the sound that advanced before that unclean beast-army like a wall of sound.

It was a great whistling. The tune was hauntingly familiar to the shocked ears of Colonel Hahmad Barsoomian.

He couldn't place it. But he knew he had heard it before. Somewhere.

Colonel Barsoomian had no idea he was listening to a thousand pink lips giving voice to the theme from the classic motion picture *Bridge over the River Kwai.*

He no longer cared. He dropped his AK-47 and dashed for an APC. The starter ground as he cursed the balky Soviet-made vehicle. Then he sent the APC careening north, driving with one hand over an ear to keep out that damnable whistling.

He had to warn his fellow Renaissance Guards that an army of the unclean was on the march.

He did not care what happened to the undisciplined PPPA. Let the infidel *khazir* army have them. It did not matter. It would take real soldiers to defend Irait from this most wicked aggression.

If that were possible.

# 37

The news was so dire, no one wanted to deliver it to Maddas Hinsein.

The Revolting Command Council sat around the table. Their president was due at any moment. The foreign minister suggested that the vice-president deliver the bad news. But since the vice-president did not speak Arabic, this was difficult to implement.

"But the infidel have rolled across the Maddas Line," said the education minister in a voice so tight a hand might have been at his throat.

"Without firing a shot," added the minister of culture. "The PPPA simply deserted their posts. The Precious Leader will be furious. Someone will be shot."

"Let us suggest that he himself shoot the PPPA," the foreign minister said suddenly. "Each one. Personally. He will like that. And it will keep him occupied."

The defense minister added his two cents. "It is a brilliant idea, but too late, alas."

"What do you mean?"

"They have been decimated by the Renaissance Guard, who cut them down as they overran guard divisions."

"Are there not any left?" asked the foreign minister.

"Only Renaissance Guard elements, and they are our last hope to hold Kuran," he was told.

Eyes met around the conference table. At one end,

Don Cooder and Vice-President Jackman exchanged uneasy glances.

"Looks like they got bad news or something," whispered Jackman.

"Looks like," Cooder said, fingering his new mustache. It was really coming in now. He hoped the Precious Leader would approve. Maybe it would impress him enough that he would not be shot, as seemed to happen a lot. He was just starting to get the hang of the job, which seemed to consist of groveling. Don Cooder had garnered extensive groveling experience during his previous career interviewing various heads of state.

"Well, we're safe," Jackman ventured.

"How you figure that?"

"I'm second from the top and you're my right-hand man."

"That didn't help the last information minister," Don Cooder pointed out.

Reverend Juniper Jackman grew very quiet.

President Maddas Hinsein stormed in a moment later.

"What news?" he demanded, taking his seat.

No one answered. Maddas pounded the table with his fist. "Report! What transpires at the front?"

"It . . . it has been overrun," said the defense minister. "Completely."

Maddas Hinsein blinked. "The Maddas Line? My pride and joy? The bulwark of Islam?"

"I am sorry, but it is true." The defense minister squeezed tears from his eyes.

Frowning, Maddas Hinsein extracted his pistol from its holster and casually shot his defense minister in the face. Everyone was impressed by the results. Not to mention splattered.

The muzzle shifted to the culture minister. "You! The Maddas Line—does it hold?"

"Yes, Precious Leader. It stands as unbreached as before," the man said quickly.

"You are lying," said Maddas Hinsein, performing a radical tracheotomy with a lead slug.

The culture minister fell off his chair gurgling. The muzzle next went to the foreign minister.

"The truth! Speak it!"

"Pigs!" bleated the foreign minister. "The Americans have been breeding with swine! Genetic mutant pig soldiers have overrun our first line of defense. Mechanized sows! Flying pigs! What Moslem can stand before such an unclean army?"

Maddas Hinsein's sad brown eyes fluttered at this report.

"Preposterous! I will spare you if you speak the truth in the next few seconds."

But . . . Precious Leader. This *is* the truth. Before Allah, I—"

The foreign minister's mustache was driven into his teeth, and his teeth through his spine by another bullet.

Vice-President Juniper Jackman would have been next, but a messenger entered at that point, crying, "Precious Leader, the Renaissance Guard! They are being destroyed!"

"By what army?"

"By our own army. Iraiti regulars have overun them in their panic to flee the advancing pig dancers."

"Dancers?"

"They appear to be dancing as they advance. And whistling."

Maddas Hinsein lifted a field telephone from under the table. It connected directly with the general in charge of Renaissance Guard forces in occupied Kuran, now Maddas Province.

Instead of an Arabic voice answering, he heard whistling. He recognized the theme from *Bridge over the River Kwai.* The Scimitar of the Arabs had no doubts that these were American pigs whistling. *Bridge over the River Kwai* was on the Iraiti forbidden-films list.

Woodenly he dropped the phone.

"There is worse news, Precious Leader," the guardsman said stiffly. "The U.S. government has declared that you are a war criminal. They say they intend to hang you until dead."

"I will not hang!" roared Maddas Hinsein. "I am the Scimitar of the Arabs. There is not a man alive who can make me hang if I do not wish to. Is that not so, my loyal ones?"

"Absolutely, Precious Leader," chorused the surviving members of the Revolting Command Council, save the vice-president and the information minister, who, not understanding Arabic, settled for staring wide-eyed into space and keeping their legs together so their bladders did not empty themselves.

"They say the Pigs of Peace, as the propaganda broadcasts call them, will cross into Irait if war criminals are not turned over to them. They are very angry over the gas attack on their computer outpost."

"Then they shall have war criminals," Maddas Hinsein announced resolutely. He gazed about the room. "Who will volunteer to surrender themselves? Those who do will go down in Iraiti history. The others will remain with me. Come, come. I know it is a difficult choice, but you are brave men."

A lot of fast thinking went on in the collective brains of the Revolting Command Council. Either option was grave. Neither was desirable. A few considered the American option, but the fear that this was a trick question, a test of loyalty, stayed them.

The minister of agriculture had the presence of mind to translate the option into English for the vice-president and the information minister.

Jackman and Cooder took only a second to decide.

"I'll do it!" said the former.

"No, I will," said the latter. "I'll gladly turn myself over to the Americans."

Their words did not have to be translated into Arabic for the benefit of Maddas Hinsein. Their eagerness to sacrifice themselves for him was plain on their infidel faces. This brought a tear to his eyes.

He came to his feet and gathered up both men in a bear hug. He kissed them on each cheek. Twice.

"You will never be forgotten," said the Scimitar of the Arabs. "Go, now. A plane will be waiting for you."

On the way out of the palace, Don Cooder said, "I can't believe the big lummox fell for it."

"Amen, brother."

As they stood outside the palace trying to hail a cab, Reverend Jackman raised a possibility that had not occurred to them before. "You don't think the U.S. will actually hang us for war criminals, do you?"

The anchor and the reverend exchanged sagging expressions.

They dashed back to the iron entrance gate, banging and shouting and begging for their old jobs back. This was reported to the president, who was forced to brush a tear from his face at the news. "Do not let them in," he added.

Then he turned to his council, saying, "I have this moment decided that I will not allow Iraiti honor to be sullied by this insult. If I cannot possess Kuran, no one may. Defense Minister—"

Maddas Hinsein looked around the table. The late defense minister's left foot had caught on the table edge. That was all of him that could be seen from a sitting position.

"Who would like to be the new defense minister?"

No one raised a hand, so Maddas Hinsein casually waved a hand in the direction of the health minister.

"You."

"I accept, O Precious Leader," said the new defense minister unhappily.

"Go forth and launch all our Scuds."

"The target, Precious Leader?"

Maddas leaned forward. His smile was sick.

"Jerusalem," he said.

An audible gasp filled the room.

"But, Precious Leader, Jerusalem is sacred."

"To the Jews. And the Christians."

"And to us. The Dome of the Rock is there. If we gas Jerusalem, not only will the infidel and the Jew be down upon us, each of our Arab neighbors will be too. Our allies."

"This is what I wish," said Maddas Hinsein firmly. "If I cannot have my way with the world, then everyone on earth must die. I have decided this. Issue the commands. Shoot any who hesitate."

"But, Precious Leader—"

"When you are done, shoot yourself," Maddas said flatly. "There will be no shirking. The hour of glory has come! Civilization was born in the glory that was Abominadad, and from here we will transform the world into a caldron of blood."

The defense minister hurried from the room.

On the way out, he bumped into Sky Bluel, who wore an unhappy expression on her well-scrubbed face. She pushed past into the council room.

"Excuse me," she said, "but I think this so-called tritium is actually a cheesy grade of uranium. I need better materials if I'm going to whip up a working neutron bomb, know what I mean?"

This was relayed to Maddas Hinsein, who invited the American girl to join him at the conference table.

"You want my advice?" she said. "Boss move."

Sky Bluel obligingly went for the seat indicated by the Iraiti president's careless gesture. It happened to be between the dead defense minister and the deceased foreign minister.

"Oh, gross! Are these guys dead?"

No one answered.

"What killed them, anyway?"

"Our Precious Leader has invited you to sit, so you must sit," said the minister of agriculture.

"I'm not sitting between two dead guys," Sky insisted. "No way. They smell and they're making uncool noises."

And since the Scimitar of the Arabs no longer needed an American nuclear expert because he expected American and Israeli nukes to rain down upon all their heads at any minute, he ordered the noisy American girl to be taken to the lowermost torture chamber to await his pleasure.

As she was dragged off, Sky Bluel hurled back the most vicious insult she could summon up.

"You're no Ho Chi Minh! You're not even a Ché Guevara!"

Sky Bluel grew silent as she was escorted to the dungeon area. Her guard happened to speak English and remarked with some relish, "I will put you in with the dead American imperalists."

"If I have to be locked up with imperialists," Sky said, "I guess I'd prefer dead ones. I feel a strong urge to meditate coming on. This whole trip is getting very, very heavy."

The guard paused at a rude door marked by a small window bisected by iron bars. A faint pounding came from the other side.

"What is this?" said the guard, putting his face to the bars.

Instantly a quartet of black arms grabbed his face, his throat, and his epaulets. He screamed, dropping a ring of keys. Sky grabbed this and shrank into a corner as the guard was methodically throttled to death.

When he was still, Sky slipped up to the bars.

"Hello, in there," she hissed. "Are you political prisoners?"

*"Yes."* The voice was dead. *"Open the door."*

"Coming right up," said Sky, fumbling for the right key.

She pulled on a thick iron ring and the door creaked open.

To her openmouthed astonishment, out stepped a woman with matted hair and skin the color of coal dust. She was nude. Her red eyes blazed in Sky's direction.

"Far out!" Sky said in a thick voice, not quite registering the lean apparition's four arms. "What did they do to you? I mean, how can I help you, you poor oppressed thing?"

The red eyes bored into her. One hand lifted, curling so that a single finger pointed at her.

*"Give me that."*

Sky touched her hair. "You mean my headband?"

*"Yes. It is my favorite color."*

"Sure," said Sky, whipping the yellow ribbon from her hair. As she held it out, she asked, "It won't cover much, you know."

*"Just your neck,"* said Kali, who fell upon Sky Bluel like an ebony spider clutching a strand of yellow webbing.

As she was slowly throttled to the cold stone floor, Sky gurgled inarticulately. In that respect, she died as she had lived.

# 38

The command went out.

All over Irait, mobile Scud launchers rumbled out of places of concealment. Crews sent their missiles lifting skyward on their rail launchers like a hundred symbols of Arab sexual prowess. Coordinates were programmed into on-board targeting computers.

More than one devout soldier, recognizing the significance of those coordinates, wept openly and cursed the name of Maddas Hinsein.

At air bases from the Kurani border to the frontier with Turkey, from Syria to the west and Iran to the east, pilots leapt into the Soviet MiG 29's and French-built F-1 Mirage fighters, as ground crews frantically affixed chemical payloads to bomb racks and wing mounts.

The flight that would send the world at last into the Red Abyss of Hell was about to be launched. At the command of one man.

It happened that Yussef Zarzour commanded the first Scud to lift off. The massive coordinated strike was supposed to launch simultaneously, but Zarzour was still flushed with the success of his elimination of the 324th Data Processing Cohort, and could not wait to taste of new glory.

Had he known that his Scud was aimed at Jerusalem, he would have instantly reprogrammed it to demolish the

Palace of Sorrows. But he was ignorant of that fateful fact.

Hunkered in the shelter of a rock outcropping, he listened for the roar of the rising missile, setting himself for the seismic blast of superheated air and exhaust gases. His fingers were jammed into his dirty ears.

The long thunder of the Scud's plume never came. Zarzour was counting off the seconds. He kept counting. The number twenty should have signified liftoff. He stopped at fifty-five.

He stuck his head up from the rocks.

The Scud simply stood there pointing to the blue sky. It had not cleared the launch rail. Smoke dribbled from the tail. It was gray and lazy.

As Yussef Zarzour watched, the Scud suddenly came apart in a flower of noise, burning rocket fuel and shrapnel.

A sharp shingle of the latter whisked his head off his neck. His crouched body didn't so much as twitch as the shrapnel executed a textbook surgical strike. It was found months later, still in a crouched position, birds pecking at the raw stump between his inert shoulders.

Other Scuds did lift off throughout Irait. They executed parabolas, loops, and arcs that would have astounded their Soviet builders.

These acrobatics terrified the gaping crew chiefs, some of whom fell victim to their own weapons as the rockets careened and tumbled, wildly out of control, back to ground with explosive results.

Scuds blew up on their rails. Or landed hundreds of kilometers short of their targets. Some never got erect. As the rails toiled skyward, they snapped as if brittle with age. In those cases, crews discovered the heavy steel rail launchers had actually crumbled as if from the elements.

In other instances, after successfully erecting, the rails collapsed due to the vibration of launch. Since the Scud was never designed for horizontal launching, this was particularly disastrous to surrounding crews, buildings, and natural rock formations.

Iraiti pilots fared no better. Mirages, towed from their revetments, suffered acute damage during that simple proceedure. Nose cones fell off. Landing gear collapsed. Bomb-laden MiG wings dropped loose at their roots, releasing nerve gases on ground crews.

A few Iraiti Air Force jets did get off the ground. Rudders and elevators came off under the G-force strain of takeoff. Wings were sheared off for no apparent reason. Canopies flew away in flight, forcing pilots to eject where they could.

More than one Iraiti pilot was doomed to ride his precision fighter down into the smoking hole that was to become his grave, cursing Soviet workmanship and Maddas Hinsein by turns.

It was as if the hand of God had interceded to save the world from one megalomaniac's nightmare ambition. For no one could understand how the entire Iraiti Air Force and its rocketry units could misfire simultaneously.

Especially President Maddas Hinsein, who shot dead the first two ministers who informed him to his face of the most crushing defeat in Iraiti history.

When he ran out of ministers to shoot, he promoted his personal driver, a corporal in the Renaissance Guard, to defense minister and had the trembling man drive him to a Scud site south of Abominadad, which had misfired but was still intact.

When the Scud crew saw the white limousine of their Precious Leader coming up the road, they formed a circle and drew their service pistols in unison. At the count of three, they opened fire on the center of the circle.

The center was empty. Their bloody bodies soon filled it.

President Maddas Hinsein stepped over the bodies

with grim unconcern. He strode up to the inert Scud, squinting at it.

There was a long black squiggle running up one side of the Scud. He had to tilt his head to make it out.

It was a name. An unfamiliar name. The script was so large it curled around the tubular rocket's body almost to the point of being unreadable, forcing the Scimitar of the Arabs to walk around the launcher in order to read it in full.

The script read: "NISEEN."

"Who is this Niseen?" roared Maddas Hinsein, shaking his fist.

"I do not know, Precious Leader," replied the new defense minister.

"Then have every man in Irait named Niseen executed at once!"

"At once, Precious Leader," said Defense Minister Niseen Ammash, who threw his ID cards out the window during the drive back to the Palace of Sorrows and swore to himself that he would go by the name of Toukan for the rest of his days.

He figured that would take him through Tuesday.

# 39

The launch plumes dappling the Iraiti landscape were visible from orbit. Central Intelligence Agency analysts counted over a thousand—which puzzled them because it was more than double the number of Scuds known to be in the Iraiti inventory.

It took hours, but they figured out that some of the flashes were not launch plumes but points of impact. All were well within the borders of Irait, another puzzle.

This intelligence was relayed to the Pentagon, which could make no sense of it, to the White House, which took great pleasure in it, and to Praetor Winfield Scott Hornworks, at that moment riding atop a Marine amphibious assault vehicle through liberated Kuran City like a pasha astride a pink elephant.

It was not obviously a Marine land vehicle, since its angular lines were concealed by a pink fiberglass shell in the shape of a fifteen-foot-high sow. It bounced along like a parade float, its squiggly tail whipping up and down.

An upright pig walked up to the sow and doffed its pink piglike gas mask.

"Sir, intelligence reports the Scud and fighter-jet threat to be completely suppressed," said the pig, actually a centurion with the Praetorian Sues, formerly the Presidential Guard.

"He did it, dang his yellow bones!" whooped Praetor Hornworks, waving a silver standard topped by an eagle and emblazoned with the letters CPQA. "That old gook did it! We liberated Kuran without suffering a single casualty. Screw taking the skies. We got total sand superiority! Sues Pacifica rules!"

"Sues Pacifica, sir?"

"The Pigs of Peace, son," Hornworks explained. "Get your snout in a Latin primer sometime. You might learn something useful."

"Does that mean we can climb out of these silly suits, sir? The men are thirsty as hell."

"Whistling up a sandstorm will do that to a centurion," said Hornworks, eyeing the horizon, which seemed to go straight up to Irait without a bump. "Start passing the canteens. It's Miller time."

"Aren't we forbidden to have alcohol, sir? This is a Moslem country, after all."

Praetor Hornworks fixed his centurion with a cold eye. "Son, if any Ay-rab so much as looks at you crossways, you rear up on your hind legs and give him a good loud oink. That'll get up his skirts worse than the sand fleas."

The centurion gave a snappy salute. "Yes, *sir*!"

Praetor Winfield Scott Hornworks returned to searching the northern horizon line. Somewhere up there, the Master of Sinanju roamed. The final phase of Operation Dynamic Eviction was in his hands. Hornworks hoped he had it in him. The old guy had looked as old as Confucius. And twice as tired. Hornworks had never seen a man look so tired. Like he had come to the end of his string, with maybe one last errand to finish before he cashed himself out.

The question was: how was he going to decapitate Maddas and his command structure without a passel of B-52's backing him up?

# 40

The government of the Islamic Republic of Iran was alerted to the impending incursion by the president of neighboring Afghanistan.

"Why are you telling us this?" asked the speaker of the Iranian Parliament suspiciously. The two nations were not known for being on friendly terms.

"So you understand the scourge coming your way is not sent by us," replied the president of Afghanistan. "We have lost enough troops to the scourge."

"Scourge? Are the Russians coming?"

"These are not Russians. The Russians refused to come to our assistance. They were smarter than us, who have thrown away two crack divisions against the scourge."

Since such a high opinion of Russian intelligence was virtually unheard-of in the Islamic world, the speaker of Iran's Parliament took the warning to heart.

"What is it you suggest we do?" he asked carefully.

"Pray to Allah that the scourge is not intent upon gobbling up your nation and only wishes to pass through."

"Gobble?"

"You will know of its approach by the trembling of the ground and the singing," the Afghan president went on. "One will bring fear to your heart and the other tears of joy to your face. The scourge itself, however, will bring ruin to your armies if they dare stand in its path."

"If it is Allah's will that this be done, who are we to challenge the will of Allah?" asked the speaker.

"I trust that was a rhetorical question," returned the Afghan president dryly. "For it would be better that you spit in Allah's eye than contemplate victory over the monster approaching your border."

"Spoken like a godless tool of the Communists," spat the speaker.

"Perhaps. But my nation is still intact. Will yours be, come the morrow?"

The line went dead.

The speaker of the Iranian Parliament went to a wall map. He picked out the point where the creature or power the Afghan had called the scourge would cross their mutual border.

He saw that the path would take this scourge through the sands of the Dasht-i-Kavir Desert, south of Tehran.

Since he did not wish to lose his republic for the sake of a useless desert, the speaker put in a call to the Iranian president, with whom he reluctantly shared power.

"Should we not defend the revolution?" demanded the president after he had heard the speaker through. "For it is truly written that submission to Allah's will is not to be avoided."

"No," the speaker said thoughtfully. "For if I read my map correctly, this scourge of the Afghans is bent upon reaching the criminal Iraiti nation."

"Allah be praised."

# 41

The city of Abominadad was the cradle of human civilization. Erected at a particularly sinuous twist of the Tigris River, it had birthed the first alphabet, the art of writing, astronomy, algebra, and a long line of kings that had included the most powerful and despotic in history.

Destroyed many times over the centuries, Abominadad had always been rebuilt. Always larger. Always to grow to greater power, more grandiose aspirations.

And while the center of earthly civilization had shifted to Persia, then Egypt, Greece, Rome, England, and, in the twentieth century, the unknown and unguessable Western land known as America, Abominadad patiently tore down her old towers and threw up new ones. She prospered, expanded, and, most important, dreamed. Waiting for the desert stars to favor her again.

In the late twentieth century, some five million Arabs dwelt in Abominadad—more human beings than had populated the young globe when her first minaret was erected in the storied days no eye living today had beheld.

Of them, no Iraiti ear had ever heard the haunting sound that swelled across the Tigris.

Yet all five million inhabitants of Abominadad felt their blood run cold when they first caught that sound. Fear clutched at every heart. Hands shook.

It was a sound, high and haunting, that they understood in their souls. It burned in their blood. It resonated in racial memories. Fathers had imitated that sound, teaching it to sons, and sons to grandsons. Although it had become diluted, imperfect, half-forgotten, every Iraiti from the mountainous Turkish border to southern salt marshes had learned to approximate the sound that keened through the dry air.

It was a call of defiance and a knell of doom.

And as it sliced the sky, pure and crystalline, it brought a startled silence from the city. The *muezzin* froze in their minarets, the call *"Allaaah Akbaaar"* dying in their suddenly tight throats. The women withdrew to their homes like black crows seeking shelter from a storm. The children sought their mothers.

And the men, who alone knew the true significance of that cosmic sound, made haste to gather up their clan.

For the first time in generations, Abominadad was about to be evacuated. Not because of the threat of falling bombs and raining missiles. Not because of pestilence. Not even because of fire.

But because of a beautiful song floating through the air.

"What is that exquisite song?" asked President Maddas Hinsein, who, because he had been orphaned young, had had no father to mimic that weirdly ethereal keening.

Receiving no answer, he turned to his defense minister, only to find the man staring down at his darkening crotch.

A puddle formed around the man's left shoe, ruining a Persian rug that months before had graced the palace of the deposed Emir of Kuran and now covered the floor of President Hinsein's office in the Palace of Sorrows. A great seven-foot bejeweled sword hung on the wall behind the man's head.

Since he could always shoot his defense minister later,

Maddas Hinsein forbore to draw his pearl-handled revolver and instead affixed a broad grin of good humor on his face. They were always disarmed by that grin, were his victims.

"Are you ill, my brother?" Maddas asked sympathetically.

The new defense minister looked up. "No, Precious Leader. I am dead."

"Come, come," said Maddas Hinsen, striding over to clap a fatherly hand on the man's quivering back. "Do not think because you have pissed on my favorite rug that I will shoot you dead."

"I wish that you would."

Maddas Hinsein's mustache and eyebrows lifted all at once. "Truly? Why, brother Arab?" he asked.

"Because it would be infinitely more merciful than what I and all of Abominadad will suffer at the hands of the authors of that song."

"Tell me more," prompted the Scimitar of the Arabs, leading the man to a window with a reassuring arm across his shoulders. "I am very interested in what you have to tell me."

The window happened to be near a spot where the rug fell short. It also overlooked a broad panorama of the city proper.

Maddas Hinsein gazed out over the city that, even in this dark hour, was his pride and joy. Nebuchadnezzar had ruled this very city. Before the evil thing had befallen him and he was exiled into the desert to eat scrub grass and consort with oxen. In the future, this sprawling metropolis would be the capital of all Dar al-Islam, the Realm of Islam.

His chest swelled with the pride he felt. A shine appeared in his moist brown eyes, making them glow like mournful stars. His fixed grin widened, and softened with true joy.

Then his eyes focused on the streets and broad avenues choked with fleeing cars and trucks. His fleshy face fell.

"My people!" Maddas Hinsein said in surprise. "Where do they go?"

"To safety, Precious Leader."

He touched his heart. "Safety? They are safe here. With me."

"They do not think so," the defense minister said quickly.

Maddas Hinsein looked down at the man's sweaty face.

"You speak boldly, for once," he said suspiciously.

"I no longer fear you, Precious Leader," answered the defense minister. He closed his eyes. "You may shoot me now."

Maddas Hinsein took the man by both shoulders. "I have no intention of shooting you. Are we not brothers?"

That has not stopped you before, the defense minister thought. Aloud he said stiffly, "If you insist."

"Then tell me: before Allah, what frightens you, brother Arab?"

The calling came again. It cut through the glass like a blade of sound wielded by *houris*.

"Before Allah," said the defense minister, his fear-sick eyes darting about the room, "that."

"But it is so beautiful."

"Only to another of the *ruh* who utter it."

"*Ruh?* I do not believe in demons."

"You will." The defense minister licked drying lips. "If you are not planning to shoot me, Precious Leader, may I shoot myself?"

"No," said Maddas Hinsein sternly. "What sound is that? Quickly, I weary of this word play."

"Mongols," croaked the defense minister.

"Speak louder."

"Mongols," repeated the defense minister, this time in a high, squeaky voice like a child whose finger had been caught in a mousetrap. "It is their *hoomei* you hear. What they call the long song."

The sad eyes of Maddas Hinsein, Scimitar of the Arabs, narrowed at the sound of the word "Mongols." There was not much schooling in his past. He knew little of modern history—one reason he had miscalculated so badly in annexing Kuran. Of ancient history, he carried in his head only the great moments in Arab pageantry, and little of the terrible fates that befell those rulers who, like himself, overreached themselves.

But he had heard of Mongols. Dimly. They dwelt in the far east. Somewhere.

"These sounds are made by Chinese?" he muttered, blinking stupidly. "The Chinese are not arrayed against us. They have been our friends. Sometimes in secret ways."

"Mongols are not Chinese," the other man said after several attempts to swallow. "The Chinese fear Mongols more than any other foe."

"They have never faced Renaissance Guardsmen," Maddas remarked confidently.

"Mongols are"—the defense minister groped for a proper comparison—"more fierce than even Turks. They nearly conquered the world once," he added in a strange voice. "Once, they vanquished Irait."

"I do not recall hearing such a tale," allowed Maddas Hinsein, a worried frown beginning to darken his features for the first time.

"They rode out of Mongolia astride their tireless ponies and laid waste to everything in their path. Those who resisted were put to the sword in cruel, merciless ways."

"And those who surrendered?" wondered President Maddas Hinsein. He noticed that the song, which had lifted again, seemed to emanate from the east. The population of Abominadad was beating a path west.

The defense minister swallowed. "Put to the sword in

even crueler ways. For the Golden Horde of Genghis Khan despised those who refused to fight even more than they did resistance to their will."

Maddas Hinsein's arm fell from his aide's shoulder as if every nerve had been severed by surgical lasers. He had heard of this Genghis. He was a mighty warrior. As famous in his way as Saladin, who had routed the Crusaders.

"Perhaps they have come to join our cause," he said hopefully.

"Perhaps," the other agreed. "But when they were last here, they besieged Abominadad."

"The city was walled in those days," said Maddas Hinsein. "How could mere horsemen successfully besiege our glorious city?"

"It is written in the histories that the caliph in those days first saw a cloud of dust in the distance."

Maddas Hinsein went to the opposite window of his office. The one that looked eastward. He did see dust. Of course, there was always dust in the air. This time of year the sandstorms and dust devils were especially fierce.

"What else?" asked the Scimitar of the Arabs, nervousness coloring his deep voice for the first time.

"The rumbling of many horses told the caliph that the fate of Abominadad was nigh."

Through the glass, through his boots and the floor beneath them, came a faint vibration. It made Maddas Hinsein's teeth click and chatter. He set them defiantly.

"What then?"

"I cannot understand you, Precious Leader," said the defense minister.

"What happened then?" shouted President Maddas Hinsein, unclenching his teeth. The floor under him was shaking now. It was a very steady shaking. Like a thunder that had rolled out of the ages.

"The hordes of Hulegu came to the Ishtar Gate."

Maddas scowled. "Hulegu? What of Genghis?"

"Genghis was dead by this time—otherwise we would not be here speaking of these matters," the trembling defense minister offered. "Genghis left behind only dust. Hulegu was sloppier."

"Go on!" urged Maddas Hinsein, noticing that the dust cloud was darkening. It was midday but the brightness of the sun was fading. The dust was very, very black now.

"Hulegu and his Mongols stormed the Ishtar Gate and overwhelmed poor, defenseless Abominadad," the defense minister went on.

"Bah! We are not defenseless now."

"Nor were they then, Precious Leader. The garrison was captured and its soldiers divided among the Mongols."

"Slavery is a fitting fate for those without the stomach to defend their nation," Maddas spat contemptuously.

"They were not enslaved," said the man. "They were divided for slaughter. The caliph was captured and forced to order his people to leave the city where they laid down their arms."

That reminded Maddas Hinsein of the teeming refugees passing beneath this window.

"Why do my people run without leave from their Precious Leader?"

"Perhaps because they have read the same histories as I," suggested the defense minister.

"What histories?" demanded Maddas Hinsein through tight teeth. The palace was shaking now. It was designed to withstand a direct missile hit. It took a lot to make such an edifice tremble. Yet he barely heard his defense minister's words of explanation.

"The ones that tell of how after the people of Abominadad surrendered, they were all put to the sword. The Tigris ran red on that evil day."

"Never mind the people!" Maddas shouted, seeing for

the first time a line of horses coming out of the desert. They looked small, the riders astride them low and squat, their wide faces as hard and unfeeling as rank upon rank of hammered bronze gongs. "Tell me of the caliph's fate!"

"Caliph al-Musta'sim was allowed to live for seventeen days, while Abominadad was sacked and burned." Tears welled up in the defense minister's jewellike eyes.

Maddas Hinsein turned, his face sagging. His eyes implored an unspoken question.

"The caliph!" Maddas roared. "What of the caliph, you ignorant dog?"

"Then they sewed him in a bag and trampled him to death under the hooves of their horses," replied the weeping defense minister. "May I die now?"

"No, you may not die!" thundered Maddas Hinsein, drawing himself up. "You are an Arab. Arabs do not lay down their lives before an enemy. Where is your courage?"

The defense minister obediently pointed to the dark wet stain on the former royal rug of the Kurani emir.

"It is there, Precious Leader," he said simply.

"There is a way out of this predicament," Maddas shouted, pacing the rug. "There is always a way. I need only think of it."

"It is too late. The thunder of Mongol doom is upon us. And our best forces are bogged down in Kuran."

Maddas Hinsein's deep brown eyes acquired a crafty light. He snapped his fingers, bringing a broad grin to his sober face.

"Contact the Americans," he said quickly. "Inform them I wish to enter into an alliance. They may have all my oil in return for protection from these bandits."

The defense minister shook his head doubtfully. "The Americans know your true colors, Precious Leader. They know how you break your promises for the sake of the moment."

"Phone Tel Aviv, then. The Zionist Entity will be happy to learn that I now regard them with respect and affection."

"That I would not do if I were the caliph of old Abominadad and it was my only hope to escape the sewn bag of death."

"Then contact the hated Kurds!" Maddas thundered. "They are almost as savage as Mongols. Perhaps they will hurl themselves into the teeth of these animals, and both armies will be wiped out!"

"How will I do that?" the defense minister asked plaintively. "The Kurds have no telephones, no radios, and no cities. They have been practically gassed out of existence."

"What traitor did that?" roared Maddas Hinsein.

"You did."

Maddas drew his scraggly black eyebrows together like burnt caterpillars mating. He fingered his mustache worriedly. It was true. He had gassed the Kurds. In all the excitement, he had almost forgotten.

"There must be some ally that will succor me," he muttered, pacing the rug. "The Russians have nuclear weapons. Whose side are they on this week?"

"I do not think even they know," the defense minister admitted truthfully.

"Where is the PLO? After all I have done for them."

"Their leadership has been decimated by your own assassins, Precious Leader."

"What of the Grand Mullahs of Islam? They will not allow a fellow Moslem leader to perish at the hands of unbelievers."

"They have declared you an enemy of God and decreed that for your crimes against Islam, you be killed and your hands cut off."

"Oh."

And out the window, rank upon rank of Mongol horsemen drew near, the pounding of their multitudinous hooves raising a black cloud that had blocked out the very moon and cast a pall over even the unquenchable spirits of President Maddas Hinsein.

He wondered if he too would end up like King Nebuchadnezzar, cast out into the hostile desert, eating tufts of dry scrub grass with the oxen and other dumb brutes.

Then, remembering the fate of Caliph al-Musta'sim, he realized the answer to that question.

Only if he were lucky.

# 42

President Maddas Hinsein fingered the wallboard control that caused the six-thousand-pound steel door to roll closed behind him.

He descended into the multilevel bunker under the Palace of Sorrows that had been made by German engineers to withstand a direct hit from everything from an H-bomb to laser cutting beams, content that no matter what happened to his unimportant populace, he would emerge alive at the end of it.

And if alive, he would be ultimately victorious.

Maddas swaggered through the maze of passages to a duplicate of his office above. All that it lacked was the Kurani emir's excellent rug.

But at least it would have the wonderful Korean sword, which Maddas personally carried, wrapped in heavy burlap to protect his fingers from the wickedly sharp blade.

He placed this on his great desk while he removed the knit khaki jersey that he had worn when he had executed the final member of his cabinet, the defense minister whose name he had already forgotten. It was stiff with blood and smeared with coagulated brain matter.

From a drawer in the desk he drew forth a long funereal black garment—a spare *abayuh.* Pulling this over his head, he allowed the fine fabric to settle down over his thick hips, which wiggled sinuously. He drew a veil over his sad brown face.

"Ahhh," sighed the Scimitar of the Arabs as the comforting fabric soothed his troubled soul. Wearing the veil was his most secret vice, kept from even his late wife. It was a relic of the days he had escaped to Egypt disguised as a woman, after the failure of a youthful coup. The *abayuh* proved to be a tension reliever more excellent than torturing Kurds.

He slipped a CD into a Blaupunkt deck. The strains of "Salome's Seven Veils" rolled over his shrouded form like waves of bedouin glory.

Throwing his hands up in the air, he began throwing his hips about, fingers snapping in syncopation.

"Mad Ass, Mad Ass," he sang in a low baritone. "I am the most crazy-assed Arab of all time."

The dry clearing of a throat caused his eyes to go wide behind his veil. In a long wall mirror he caught a reflective glimpse of a wispy presence in white.

Maddas Hinsein wheeled.

Standing in the doorway, hands tucked in the sleeves of a pale kimono, was a tiny Oriental man who looked as old as the Prophet himself.

"What are you doing here?" Maddas demanded, yanking off his veil. It did not matter that the man had discovered him in an *abayuh*. They were entombed together in the bunker. The old man would not live to reveal the secrets of Maddas.

"I am Chiun," he said quietly. "I entered with you."

"I entered alone."

"Did not your shadow follow you in?" asked the old one.

"Of course. But what has that to do with you?"

"I am your shadow," said the old Oriental, padding forward on silent white sandals. He might have been a little yellow ghost in a shroud of bone. His eyes were unreadable slits.

"Who are you really, old one?" Maddas demanded, slipping one hand into a gap in the folds of his black garment. It closed about his ivory-handled revolver.

"I am Chiun, Reigning Master of Sinanju."

"That title means nothing to me," Maddas spat.

The little wisp of a man stopped not six feet away from the Scimitar of the Arabs.

"I am he who trained the assassin who fell into your power," he said without emotion.

"The American?"

"His name was Remo. And he was the greatest pupil a Master of Sinanju could ever have."

"This Sinanju, why have I never heard of it?"

"Perhaps," said the old man, "because you are ignorant and unread."

Maddas Hinsein knew an insult when he heard one. The pistol came out like a viper's head, muzzle zeroing in on the Oriental's sunken chest.

"You would not shoot me, an old man," the Master of Sinanju said simply.

"Why not? I have shot so many." And Maddas laughed.

"Because I have seen fit to present you with one of the treasures of the House of Sinanju, the finest house of assassins ever to walk this ancient land."

A yellow claw of a hand emerged from the joined white kimono sleeves to gesture to the seven-foot-long sword lying swathed in burlap on the desktop.

"You! You sent this fine blade to me?"

"Yes," said the Master of Sinanju, padding up to the weapon. "I trust you have treated it with respect, for it has been in my family for over two thousand years."

"You say you are an assassin," Maddas asked, interest silvering his suspicious tone.

The one called Chiun drew himself up proudly. "No, I am *the* assassin. The last of my line."

"I have need of an assassin," Maddas said thoughtfully. "The American President has caused me much trouble. I would like him killed. Could you do this?"

"Easily," said the Master of Sinanju, carefully laying the burlap folds aside to expose the gleaming blade. He examined the rubies and emeralds on the hilt with a critical eye.

Maddas Hinsein absorbed this answer with interest. "Could you assassinate the American President with that very sword and return it to me with the President's blood upon the blade?"

"With the President's head impaled upon the tip of the blade, were it my wish to please you so."

Maddas Hinsein's brown eyes glowed with pleasure. "It would please me greatly. I think we can do business, Master of . . . what was that name?"

"How quickly they forget," said the Master of Sinanju. "Bong must be doubly shamed that his service has made no impression on you Mesopotamians."

"Names do not matter," Maddas said impatiently. "Only deeds. Will you cut off the President's head with that sword for me, or not?"

"No." The old Oriental's voice was distant. He did not look up from his examination.

Maddas Hinsein was not used to the word "no." It startled him so much that instead of shooting the old man then and there, he sputtered a question: "Why not?"

"Because this sword is reserved for the execution of common criminals, not dispatching emperors," said the Master of Sinanju, who laid careful hands upon the hilt. He seemed only to touch it, and the blade lifted into the air as if weightless.

But Maddas Hinsein knew full well that it was not weightless. He had worked up a sweat carrying it, and the Scimitar of the Arabs was built like the Bull of Bashan.

"Then how would you kill the President?" he asked.

"With the only proper instrument—my hands," replied Chiun.

"I would accept this," said Maddas Hinsein, thinking the old Oriental meant slow strangulation.

"But I would not," said the Master of Sinanju, turning to face the Scimitar of the Arabs, the weapon held balanced before him, the flared tip less than a foot from Maddas' still-sweaty face. He could not believe the little man possessed such strength.

"There is not enough gold on the face of the earth to entice me to work for one such as you," the old man went on in a tone whose coldness matched that of the blade. "I may be the last of my line, a childless old man, but I still have my pride."

Maddas Hinsein blinked stupidly. That was a second no. Did this unbeliever not comprehend with whom he was treating?

"I demand that you work for me!" he roared, cocking his pistol.

"And I refuse."

"I do not understand. If you do not wish to sell your services to the Scimitar of the Arabs, why did you send me such a magnificent sword?"

"Because," said the Master of Sinanju, drawing the blade back over his shoulder with a sharp whisk of steel cutting air, "it was too heavy to carry."

Maddas Hinsein registered the abrupt drawing back of the blade. His first thought was to pull the trigger at once. No conscious thought was involved in this snap decision. It was pure reflex.

But it came too late.

For as his brain processed the first danger signal, the old Master of Sinanju swept the blade around. His sandaled feet left the floor. And the old man became a floating flower of spinning skirts, with the sword becoming a long pistil of flashing silver beneath the overhead lights.

Maddas Hinsein realized the stroke had completed itself when the Master of Sinanju alighted on his feet, his back to him, the sword momentarily lost to his sight.

He felt the soft breeze of the blade's passing. But he knew that it had accomplished nothing. He had felt nothing, save for that gentle breeze. His eyes still saw. His feet still stood firmly, supporting his strong body.

"You missed," Maddas Hinsein's brain commanded his tongue to taunt. But what came out of his throat instead was a bubbling sound oddly unlike human speech.

And as the Master of Sinanju turned to face him once more, the long blade came up before his unreadable Oriental face. The tip was scarlet with gore, and as it lifted ceilingward, blood ran down it like cough syrup.

Out of the corner of his eyes, the Scimitar of the Arabs caught sight of his own throat in the long wall mirror. A thin red line was visible there. It seemed to go around to the back of his neck. As his eyes grew startled, the line exuded blood like more thick cough syrup dripping from a glass jar rim.

"My son has been avenged," said the Master of Sinanju coldly.

They were the last words Maddas Hinsein ever heard in life.

His legs finally got the message that no more commands would ever come from his disconnected brain. They buckled at the knees. And as he fell, his head, severed so expertly that no vertebra was injured by the razorlike blade, so swiftly that the stump to his neck kept it balanced in place, simply fell off like a shaggy hat.

The Scimitar of the Arabs felt nothing. But before the light went out in his moist eyes, his tumbling head caught sight of his falling body and the ugly red orifice that was his exposed neck.

A single tear escaped his right eye.

It was the only tear ever shed over the passing of Mad-

# 43

On the roof of the Palace of Sorrows, Kali danced.

Clasping her mate, her lover, and her dancing partner all in one to her corpse-black bosom, she turned and spun. Her naked feet made dry rustling sounds on the limestone roof, like the dead leaves of autumn skittering along pavement.

She led, because her dancing partner hung limp in her four-limbed embrace. His slipper-clad feet dragged uselessly. His head hung low, bobbing on a boneless neck like that of a strangled chicken.

*"Dance! Why do you not dance, lover?"* Kali whispered. *"I need for you to dance. For without your mighty feet moving in concert with mine, dancing the Tandava, this world of woe will toil on as before. Dance, O Red One. The Red Abyss awaits us both."*

Though no reply came from her mate's blackened lips, she danced on, her limbs shaking and quivering in death throes that would never end.

Tears flowed from Kali's blood-red eyes. The tears were a poisonous whitish-yellow, like pus. She was thinking of all the hot fluids she would drink from the Caldron of Blood, if only Shiva would lead.

# 44

Chiun, Reigning Master of Sinanju, ascended to the roof of the Palace of Sorrows to watch the fall of Abominadad by starlight.

He found instead a macabre dance, and the body of his dead pupil clasped in the scorpion's grip of the demoness that, as much as the Arab tyrant Maddas, had brought him to the end of all happiness.

As she went through her impotent motions, Kali's scarlet eyes stared blindly through him. She might have been oblivious of all the universe.

Yet she spoke. *"Begone, old one. There is nothing for you here."* Her voice was akin to a death rattle.

"This is the body of my son, whom I now claim," said the Master of Sinanju in an austere voice.

Kali expelled a rude laugh. *"If he will not dance, then I shall split his bones, lick of his marrow, and depart this body to await the next avatar of Shiva."*

The Master of Sinanju noticed the palsied twitching of her black features, the shivering of her limbs. She almost dropped her limp consort, whose head lolled so pitifully. Her anchorless head, too, whipped from side to side in her mad gyrations. They were two corpses dancing in a mockery of life.

The sight filled Chiun with the ice of bitterness.

Twenty years of love and discipline, and it had come to this sick end. He lifted his voice.

"Though you are Kali the Terrible, and I but an old man," Chiun warned, "I will expend the last of my essence before I allow you to despoil my son's body further."

Kali laughed mockingly. *"You are but a mortal husk, bereft of virility, devoid of power. I will gnaw the living flesh from your old bones if you do not begone."*

"Bare your teeth, then, harlot," said the Master of Sinanju, advancing, the great sword of Sinanju before him. "For you face a fury more implacable than the hell from which you sprang."

Kali swept to a stop, Remo's head bobbing ghoulishly. Her blind scarlet eyes fixed upon the old Korean. A corpse grin twitched her lips into a death rictus.

"*I hunger for blood, but living flesh may suffice,*" she said, dropping Remo into a pitiful pile. Her quivering arms lifted in unison, like an optical illusion.

"And I yearn for vengeance," said Chiun, sweeping in.

The Master of Sinanju shook his pipestem arms free from billowing kimono sleeves, the better to wield his mighty blade.

Kali's outspread arms closed like a Venus's-flytrap.

The sword's spade-shaped point clicked against a dead black forearm. The Master of Sinanju thought this would be the final blow he was destined to land in life.

But it was not. A black hand, like a spider descending a strand of silk, simply dropped off the attacking wrist.

Recovering his balance, Chiun slashed defensively.

An elbow splintered like a dried tree branch, causing the lower left arm of the demon Kali to suddenly hang down at a crazy, useless angle, as if hinged.

*"Aiee!"* cried the demon. And her bloodless stump descended for the Master of Sinanju's bald head.

Chiun planted a foot with a hard stamp, pivoted, and

using the centrifugal force of the moving blade, flicked away from the blow. He felt its breeze. But there was no force behind it.

Withdrawing several paces, he turned to face anew his opponent. A wan smile brought grim humor to his cold hazel eyes.

"You are mighty, O Kali. But your host is not. The girl's sinews are poisoned from the Arab's death gas. She is dying. Just as my Remo has perished. You will join him in death."

And he laid aside his great weapon. It was weighing him down. He was still not recovered from his long ordeal of water and undeath.

*"I will kill you first!"* screamed Kali. Yellowed teeth bare, she sprang at him like a dog.

Chiun darted from the lunge, hurling a taunt over his shoulder.

"You will kill me never, carrion thing," he spat. "You were born dead and you will die forever."

*"I will eat you!"*

Sweeping around, the Master of Sinanju paused only to take up Kali's severed hand. It was cold to the touch. Still, it twisted with tarantula animation.

"Eat you this!" called Chiun, hurling the member in the face of his attacker.

Kali screamed anew. Blood oozed from the corners of her mouth, as if the lungs had ruptured from the very violence of her cry. She caught the hand and began to gnaw upon it like a bone.

*"I will consume your hands,"* she said through a mouthful of her own fingers. *"Just as I consume my own."*

"Only a cannibal speaks empty words through a full mouth," Chiun jeered.

At that, Kali the Terrible threw away the fingerless hand and came at him screaming.

Chiun stood his ground, his eyes resolute, his thoughts cold.

*Yes. Come, Kali. Come to your doom*, he told himself. And he set himself to flick from her path so that Kali would hurl herself to her own death.

Kali undoubtedly would have done exactly that, except for one obstacle—the cold corpse of Remo Williams. He lay in her path. One of her naked feet stubbed Remo's unresponsive head.

Kali stumbled.

And like a bear trap that had been sprung, Remo's arms lifted, digging deep into the cold dead flesh of her legs.

*"You tricked me!"* Kali howled. *"You live!"*

*"And you die,"* a remorseless voice returned, beginning to drag her down to him.

As Chiun watched, his wrinkled features twisting in horror, the lolling head of his pupil strained upward on its unstable neck. Three eyes burned in his face. They were as black as balls of polished ebony. They locked with those of Kali, and the mouth, roaring, snapped and snarled at Kali's astonished face with the fury of a wild dog. The third eye began to glow, emitting a pulsing purplish beam of light.

Inexorably, Kali was wrestled to the ground. Shiva—for that was the true name of the entity that animated the remains of Remo Williams, Chiun understood—assumed a superior position, straddling the kicking, screaming corpse-thing. The purple beam bathed it like hard radiation.

*"What are you doing?"* Kali screamed, averting her face from the awful light. *"I only wanted to dance! This is our shared destiny!"*

*"My hour has not yet come,"* Shiva said in metallic tones. *"The day of the Tandava has not yet dawned. You desire blood? I give you bile."*

And with that, Shiva's mouth yawned to its fullest and

began extruding a black bile that was like cold tar streaked with blood.

The viscous matter poured over Kali's unprotected face. She kicked, she fought, howling like a cur. But in the end her nerve-damaged limbs lacked the power to resist.

Quivering and twitching, she subsided.

As Chiun watched, true fear a cold stone in his belly, Shiva dismounted his consort. He turned slowly. The three black eyes seemed to regard the Master of Sinanju like a doom.

"I do not fear you, Supreme Lord," Chiun said in a quavering voice.

*"Then you are not worthy to call yourself a Master of Sinanju,"* Shiva intoned.

Chiun swallowed. "What is your will?"

Shiva raised both hands to his forehead. They swept down to his thighs like a benediction. *"That this fleshly throne remain whole until I claim the right to sit upon it,"* he said.

Chiun's facial hair quivered. "Remo is not dead?" he gasped. His eyes went round and unbelieving.

*"The gas of death is strong, but my will is stronger."*

Chiun indicated the prostrate form of Kali. "What of her?"

*"She has tasted the excretions that, now purged, allow my avatar to breathe the air of this realm anew."*

The Master of Sinanju trembled, and fought back welling tears.

"Give me back my son, O Shiva, and any wish you desire, I will swear to fulfill."

*"Remember that vow, Sinanju,"* said Shiva. *"You may come to regret it. But on this day, in this hour, I need only to return to Chidambarum, the center of the universe, where I sleep."*

Chiun nodded. It was more than he could ever have

dreamed. A lump rose in his throat and the air coming into his lungs was inexplicably hot.

Then, assuming a lotus position on the limestone roof, Shiva the Destroyer laid his wrists upon his knees and closed all three eyes. A wave of color, like the wind worrying sailcloth, rippled over the flesh of Remo Williams. Another. The slaty color began to fade. Magically, the lopsided head reoriented itself to the vertical, the livid blue bruise of the throat lessening, fading, growing pink and healthy once more.

Remo Williams opened his uncomprehending brown eyes. They blinked, focused, and seemed to accept the pale vision that was the Master of Sinanju standing before him.

"Little Father . . ." he began, his voice a bullfrog croak.

Chiun said nothing. He could not. His every thought was focused on holding back unseemly tears.

"I thought you were . . . dead," Remo said slowly, seeming not to know where he was. He looked around. At every point of the compass, smoke lifted into the intensely black sky, and fires raged.

"Is this . . . the Void?" Remo asked tightly. "The last thing I remember was killing Maddas Hinsein. Then Kimberly grabbed me by the . . ."

His gaze suddenly alighted on the prostrate form of Kimberly Baynes, only a yard away.

"Is she dead too?"

Before the Master of Sinanju could summon up an answer, the blackened arms of Kali flung upward. Her spine coiled and her legs jackknifed. Her tottering body came erect, surviving arms outflung as if for balance.

"What's this?" Remo asked nervously.

"A gift," said the Master of Sinanju, stepping up to the creature as it pawed slime from its matted hair and face. The sounds coming forth were confused and muffled. "The Supreme Lord has offered Sinanju an opportunity to extract full vengeance."

"Hold it!" Remo warned, trying to get to his feet. "She's more dangerous than you think." His legs, locked in a lotus position, were unresponsive, as if nerve-dead.

"Do you hear me, O Kali?" Chiun demanded, ignoring his pupil.

*"I will eat you!"* Kali roared, trying to see through the dripping slime.

"Perhaps. But first I have a riddle for you."

*"What?"*

"What has three arms and screams?"

*"I do not know, foolish old man. Nor do I care."*

"Little Father!" Remo shouted, uncrossing his legs by hand. "Don't take her on alone!" His eyes were wide with worry.

The Master of Sinanju lashed out with a stiff-fingered strike, knocking the maimed arm of Kali loose from its socket. It fell with a *plop*.

Kali screamed. Her three surviving arms waved.

"Since you did not solve that one, I have another," Chiun went on calmly. "What has but two arms and screams?"

Kali obviously guessed the answer to that one, because her upper arms—the unimpaired ones—reached for the Master of Sinanju's face.

Chiun knocked her legs out from under her and grasped the swinging broken arm as she fell. The arm tore free like cloth ripping.

"I got one," Remo said, finally finding his feet. He strode over Kali's almost-normal form and asked, "What has no arms and flies?"

"And sprouts feathers in flight?" added Chiun.

Remo blinked. "Feathers?"

"Feathers," said Chiun, nodding.

His brow wrinkling around his closed third eye, Remo

Williams set one foot on Kali's bloated stomach. He grabbed her wrists and exerted pressure.

They came loose like cooked turkey drumsticks and, flinging them one way, Remo drop-kicked the maimed armless shell that was Kali in another.

Howling unimaginable curses, Kali described a shallow parabola over the Palace of Sorrows.

At the apex of her flight, she acquired a sudden halo of feathered shafts. They seemed to spring from her body like porcupine quills. But in fact, several plainly impaled her head and vitals, entering from one direction and emerging from the other.

Kali plummeted like a stricken bird. Her howl followed her down. When she hit the ground, she splintered. She didn't move until a group of men carrying great war bows descended upon her. And then she moved only because they flung her dead corpse into the nearby banks of the Tigris River, which was already running red with the blood of Iraiti soldiers.

Remo watched this from the palace parapet.

"We're in Abominadad, right?" he asked Chiun.

"Correct."

"Then why do I see Mongols down below?"

"Because you do."

Remo was silent a long moment. "Are those your Mongols or mine?" he asked at last.

"They are *our* Mongols," said Chiun, suppressing a smile as his proud eyes searched his son's face.

Boldbator Khan rode up to the Master of Sinanju and his pupil, his broad countenance beaming and blood-spattered. He dismounted his white pony, which dropped excrement with Herculean abandon. Boldbator wore a long *del* of blue brocade.

*"Sain Baina,"* Master of Sinanju," he said gruffly.

Chiun acknowledged the hail with a formal, "*Sain Baino.*

"What're you guys doing here?" asked Remo, ever the informal.

"We followed the Seven Giants as our Master bade us."

"Seven Giants?"

Boldbator Khan of the New Golden Horde pointed a stubby finger into the night sky, where the Big Dipper shone. Remo counted seven stars and said, "Oh. We call it the Big Dipper."

"Everyone knows that it is really the Seven Giants." Boldbator addressed the Master of Sinanju. "We searched in vain for the Ishtar Gate, O friend of the old days."

"The barbarians never rebuilt it since you last visited their land," Chiun supplied. "Laziness, no doubt."

Another Mongol came running up, dragging something long and limp in one hand. He wore a black leather vest and his face resembled a weather-beaten brass gong.

"Remo! It is good to see you again, White Tiger."

"Hyah, Kula. What's with the freaking bag?"

Kula the thief lifted a long canvas bag. "It is for the freaking caliph," he said proudly.

"Not much of a present," Remo noted. "Looks empty."

Kula smiled happily, saying, "Soon it will not be."

"Where is the evil one?" asked Boldbator.

"Dead," said Chiun. "I have dispatched him."

The moon faces of the two Mongols collapsed into expressions so tragic they were almost comical.

"The horses will be disappointed," said Bolbator. Kula threw away the bag with a muttered curse.

"Am I missing something here?" Remo wondered.

"It is a fine Mongol tradition," Chiun explained. "One sews up the offending monarch in a bag and tramples out his life under the hooves of wild horses."

"If we're talking about Maddas Hinsein, it sounds good to me," Remo allowed. "Except I got him." He frowned. "Didn't I?"

"That he has been dealt with is all that matters, not proper credit," Chiun sniffed.

"If you say so," said Remo, tearing a length of scarlet silk from his disheveled harem pants and using it to wipe his brow. To his surprise, he encountered a round bump like a pigeon's egg.

"What the heck is this?" he demanded.

"Do not touch it!" Chiun said, slapping Remo's hands away like those of a child. "We will deal with that later."

"Hey, is that any way to act during a family reunion?"

"There would not have been need of a reunion had you not been so reckless in your ways," Chiun scolded. "Your obtuseness has caused me much suffering. How could you not comprehend the gesture my essence made as it appeared before you? Even Smith understood this."

"Bully for Smith. Where the hell were you the last three months—hiding? I thought you were dead."

"You only wished I was dead. You coveted my Mastership."

"Bulldooky!"

"And you never informed the village of my demise."

Remo folded his arms. "*What* demise? You aren't dead."

"We will discuss this later," Chiun flared, one eye darting to the interested Mongol faces. "After the company has left."

"If this is a party," Remo said, looking down at the ruins of Abominadad, "I'd hate to see these guys at a riot. No offense."

"None taken." Kula beamed, nocking an arrow and letting it fly in Remo's direction. It whizzed by Remo's ear.

A Renaissance Guardsman, picking his way through some rubble, caught the shaft square in the eye. He screamed like a piano wire snapping. It was that short.

"This is good sport," said Kula, grinning.

"Looks like war to me," Remo muttered, checking his ear. It was still there.

"Yes, good sport. If you do not mind, we have many Arabs to massacre." They started off.

"Spare the women and children," warned Chiun.

"Of course. If we kill them too, then our descendants will have no sport in the centuries to come. They will curse our memories. Better that the Arabs curse us while we live. We will not have to listen to them after we are with our ancestors."

Laughing, they slipped away into the night.

"Nice guys," Remo said dryly.

"They are true friends of Sinanju." Chiun turned. "Have you no questions to ask of me?"

Remo pretended to think. "Yeah, just one."

"And that is?"

"Did they ever explain who killed Laura Palmer?"

## 45

"It was an owl named Bob," said Harold W. Smith with a straight face.

Remo laughed with surprise. "That's pretty funny," he said. "I didn't know you had a sense of humor."

It was the next morning. They were in the Royal Emiri Palace in liberated Kuran City. Remo had been briefed by Smith, who had flown to Hamidi Arabia to take charge of Reverend Juniper Jackman and Don Cooder, both of whom had been discovered hiding in a closet of the Palace of Sorrows.

As vice-president of Irait and the highest-ranking survivor of the Revolting Command Council, Reverend Jackman had formally surrendered the nation to the Master of Sinanju.

Immediately Don Cooder had begun pestering him for an interview. Jackman had refused on the grounds that he had too much on his mind. With an actual elected office under his belt and the presidential sweepstakes only a year away, he would make a formal announcement later. After the war-crimes tribunal.

Remo had slipped up behind them and, applying pressure to nerve centers, made them limp enough to be carried out of Irait.

That had been the day before. This was now.

"I am speaking the truth," Smith said flatly.

A decurion in a pink gasproof suit, his swinish gas mask hanging from his web belt, entered the throne room.

"The transport has arrived, sir."

"I don't suppose anyone wants to explain why the U.S. Army is tricked out like Porky Pig these days?" Remo wanted to know.

No one did, so Remo wrote it off to the vagaries of the all-volunteer army. He had been a marine. Remo did understand that Kuran had been taken without a shot being fired. Sheik Fareem and Prince Imperator Bazzaz were in the capital, Nemad, claiming the lion's share of credit. Officially, Washington had decided not to contradict this boast. The truth would have been impossible to support.

"Did you bring my ice?" Remo asked the orderly, for some inexplicable reason called a decurion.

"Here, sir."

Remo accepted the cube in a handkerchief and applied it to the lump of flesh on his forehead.

"You know," he murmured unhappily, "I don't think this swelling is going down at all."

"We will deal with that back in America," Chiun said.

"They don't have ice back in America?" Remo asked.

"Hush!" Chiun snapped.

"Why do I get the impression everyone is holding something back from me?" Remo said suspiciously.

"Because we are," said Chiun flatly.

Praetor Winfield Scott Hornworks barged in at that point, and when he saw Chiun, a bearlike grin broke over his broad face.

"Imperator Chiun!" he bellowed.

Remo almost dropped his ice pack. "Imperator?"

"You should hear what's going on up in Irait! The Kuranis have grabbed a hunk of their southern frontier. The Syrians have swept in to the Euphrates. The Iranians grabbed a slice of the east, and the Turks are taking back all the land they lost back when the Ottoman Empire broke apart. The way it's going, all that's gonna be left of Irait will be Abominadad and some suburbs, and the Kurds are sure to lay claim to that once the Mongols get through picking it over. I gotta hand it to you, using the Kurds and Mongols means we ain't ever gonna hear a squawk outta Irait again."

"What did the Kurds do?" Remo asked.

"They wrote their names on the Spuds," Chiun supplied.

"Potatoes?"

"No, he means Maddas' Scud missiles. Here . . ." Praetor Hornworks pulled an LME tube out of a slash pocket and tossed it to Remo.

Remo looked it over and said, "A Magic Marker, right?"

"Naw, it's an LME. Stands for liquid-metal-embrittlement agent. You smear some of it on any metal or alloy, and faster than corn through a cow, it breaks it down like invisible rust. Metal fatigue equals catastrophic failure. When ol' Maddas launched his rockets and planes, they up and discombobulated." He paused. "There's only one downside."

"And what is that?" asked Harold Smith.

"We not only chased all the Iraitis out of Kuran, but the Kuranis too. They all lit out for Bahrain. And nobody can find the emir to give the country back to. There's rumors he's off buying up half of Canada."

Hornworks suddenly noticed Smith's three-piece suit. "Are you CIA?" he asked.

"No." Smith pretended to adjust his glasses. He kept his hand over his face in a suspicious manner.

"You sure? You got 'spook' written all over you. I dealt with you CIA types all during the Nam thing."

"I think it is time that we depart," said Smith uncomfortably.

"Before you do," Hornworks said, turning to Chiun and coming to attention, "I just want to say that you are the finest officer I ever served under. And that includes my dear departed daddy."

"Officer?" Remo said.

Praetor Hornworks saluted smartly. The Master of Sinanju returned the salute with a deep formal bow.

Remo watched all this in growing confusion.

"Maybe this will start to make sense after the swelling has gone down," he grumbled.

The strange looks on the faces of Harold W. Smith and Chiun caused him to doubt that statement, but he shoved the doubt into the back of his mind. The nightmare was over. Everyone who mattered to him had gotten through it alive. Everyone who deserved to die, had.

Remo Williams felt a nervous exultation quivering in his solar plexus like butterflies of promise.

His good mood carried him through the fifteen-hour flight in a C-5 Galaxy.

"When we get home," Remo said, lying in a webbing net, his hands clasped behind his head in contentment, "I'm going to bake you a rice cake, Little Father. With a hundred candles."

"Why?"

"For your birthday. You're a hundred now."

"I am not!" Chiun snapped.

Remo sat up. "Then what was all that phony crap you dished out last spring?"

"That was true crap," Chiun retorted. "But I have missed my *kohi*, therefore I have not properly achieved the venerated age. Since Masters of Sinanju celebrate no birthdays between the ages of eighty and one hundred, I must remain forever young."

"Bull. You're a hundred."

"I am only eighty," said the Maste of Sinanju firmly. "Remember this. Any assertion to the contrary is a canard."

They argued this point for the remainder of the flight.

Remo Williams didn't care. Smiling contentedly, he let Chiun's carping and complaining wash over him like a reviving surf. All was right with the world. Nothing this bad could ever happen to them again, he was certain.

# Epilogue

Miss Lapon of the Hutchison Elementary School in suburban Toronto watched the six-year-olds file into the room.

"Welcome to kindergarten," Miss Lapon said brightly.

The children laughed and giggled. It would take a while to settle them down at their miniature tables, so she went to a cabinet, returning with colorful cardboard cans heavy with Play-Doh.

"For our first day, we're going to work in clay," she announced, setting a can on each table.

"Yay!" the children cried. A little blond girl with sparkling cornflower-blue eyes put her hands over her mouth, suppressing bubbling laughter.

After Miss Lapon had finished passing out the Play-Doh and the children had settled down to kneading and shaping the pastel claylike matter, she went among them to see what their young imaginations were producing.

Not much that an adult mind could recognize, Miss Lapon was not surprised to see. But that was not the purpose of this first-day exercise. Miss Lapon was looking for students having difficulty with motor coordination. It was important to spot the troubled ones early.

One little girl—it was the one who had been giggling earlier—had found a corner all to herself and was industriously pushing and pulling a sickly green lump of Play-Doh into a surprising anthropomorphic shape.

It looked to Miss Lapon's practiced eye like a squatting earth-mother figure, similar to those found in ancient Sumerian archaeological sites.

Except that this earth mother had six spidery arms.

Miss Lapon bent over her. "And how are you coming?"

The serious little girl didn't react at first.

"I asked," repeated Miss Lapon, thinking she had found a hearing-impairment problem, "how are you doing, little girl?"

The girl started. Her eyes focused. Miss Lapon made a mental note: strong powers of concentration.

"I'm almost done finishing her," the little girl said.

Miss Lapon smiled encouragement. "Very nice. Does she have a name?"

"Kali."

"Cally. That's a nice name. And what is *your* name?"

"Freya, daughter of Jilda," said the little blond girl with the cornflower-blue eyes.

Miss Lapon's eyes shone with amusment. "Don't you have a last name, Freya?"

A serious cloud passed over the childish features. "I don't think so," Freya admitted.

"No? Don't you have a daddy?"

The eye lit anew. "Oh, yes."

"What is your daddy's name?"

"His name," Freya said with childish pride, "is Remo."